"Ms. Douglas brings the reader a heroine (Maggie Skerritt) we can empathize with and a mystery we can sink our teeth into."
—*Rendezvous Reviews* on *Pelican Bay*
by Charlotte Douglas

"I have a prediction, Maggie...."

Bill stood, set my mug aside and pulled me to my feet.

"What does Swami Malcolm see in my future?"

"You're spending the night on a boat with a tall, dark man."

"Dark?"

"Well, suntanned, at least. But just because there's snow on the roof doesn't mean there's no fire in the furnace."

I couldn't resist teasing him. "You know what else they say?"

He tugged me closer. "What?"

"That by thirty-five you get your head together and your body starts falling apart."

"I don't feel a day over twenty," he said with an irresistible grin, "and I'd guess that you're just over eighteen."

"Why eighteen?"

"Because that makes what I have in mind legal."

He kissed me then, and all thoughts of murders and cold cases disappeared.

Charlotte Douglas

USA TODAY bestselling author Charlotte Douglas, a versatile writer who has produced over twenty-five books, including romances, suspense, Gothics and even a *Star Trek* novel, has now created a mystery series featuring Maggie Skerritt, a witty and irreverent homicide detective in a small fictional town on Florida's Central West Coast.

Douglas's life has been as varied as her writings. Born in North Carolina and raised in Florida, she earned her degree in English from the University of North Carolina at Chapel Hill and attended graduate school at the University of South Florida in Tampa. She has worked as an actor, a journalist and a church musician and taught English and speech at the secondary and college level for almost two decades. For several summers while newly married and still in college, she even manned a U. S. Forest Service lookout in northwest Montana with her husband.

Married to her high school sweetheart for over four decades, Douglas now writes full-time. With her husband and their two cairn terriers, she divides her year between their home on Florida's Central West Coast—a place not unlike Pelican Bay—and their mountaintop retreat in the Great Smokies of North Carolina.

She enjoys hearing from readers, who can contact her at charlottedouglas1@juno.com.

CHARLOTTE DOUGLAS

SPRING
BREAK

SPRING BREAK

copyright © 2006 by Charlotte H. Douglas

i s b n 0 3 7 3 8 8 0 8 3 9

This edition published by arrangement with Harlequin Books S.A.

® and TM are trademarks of the publisher. Trademarks indicated with
® are registered in the United States Patent and Trademark Office, the
Canadian Trade Marks Office and in other countries.

TheNextNovel.com

PRINTED IN U.S.A.

From the Author

Dear Reader,

In West Central Florida, spring and fall often arrive at the same time. In late February, as azaleas in dazzling colors burst into bloom and the air is laden with the scent of orange blossoms and confederate jasmine, deciduous trees drop their leaves. This juxtaposition of rebirth and the end of life is also reflected in the influx of college students to beach communities, where they vie with senior citizens for parking places and spaces on the sand.

This spring, as Maggie Skerritt launches her new career as a private investigator and plans her approaching marriage to Bill Malcolm, a ghost from her past has her looking back to a cold case that has haunted her for sixteen years. In this time of rebirth and renewal, Maggie finds herself surrounded, not only by young people on spring break but by death, as well. But Maggie, with the help of Bill and her former partner Adler, is determined to prevail. Enjoy spring break in Pelican Bay!

Happy reading!

Charlotte Douglas

Darcy Wilkins skidded into my office early Monday morning and closed the door. I looked up in alarm. Darcy, in all her years as a police dispatcher, had never lost her cool. And in the few weeks she'd served as receptionist for Pelican Bay Investigations, she'd been a model of efficiency and decorum. Today, however, she had the wild and crazy look of a die-hard rock 'n' roll fan who had just sighted Elvis, alive and well.

"You okay?" I asked.

"Maggie." Her voice was breathless, her brown cheeks flushed, her eyes wide and bright. "You'll never guess who's asking to see you."

Why people tell you that you can't do something, then wait for you to do it, I've never understood. "Okay, I give up."

"Jolene Jernigan!"

I drew a total blank.

Darcy must have guessed by the look on my face. "You don't know who she is."

"Haven't a clue."

"You don't watch daytime television?"

"Not if I can help it."

Darcy shook her head. "Jolene Jernigan has been the star of *Heartbeats* for more than forty years."

"*Heartbeats*? Is that a fitness show?"

I'd once caught Caroline, my older sister, sweating to the oldies with Richard Simmons, but I'd never heard of Jolene Jernigan.

Darcy looked at me as if I'd been raised in a barn. "It's the number-one soap opera on television. I watched it every day when I worked night shifts. Now that I'm working days, I have to record it."

"So what's this Jolene doing in Florida? Aren't soaps broadcast live from either New York or L.A.?"

"Her character's in a coma with her face bandaged because of an auto accident. Maybe she has a stand-in for a while."

"Did Jolene say why she's here in Pelican Bay?"

Darcy shook her head and made a *tsking* noise.

"For a detective, you don't know much. She owns a fabulous vacation home on Pelican Beach."

"And she wants to see me?"

"She says it's urgent."

I glanced at my bare desktop and my day planner devoid of appointments. "I suppose I can work her in."

"Don't forget to ask for an advance." Darcy ducked out the door.

She was right to remind me. After twenty-two years as a police officer, I wasn't yet accustomed to the business details of running a private investigation firm. I preferred that Bill Malcolm, my fiancé and partner in crime, so to speak, handle money matters, but he was in Sarasota on another case.

Through the open windows of our recently acquired second-floor office, I could hear the traffic idling on Main Street as it backed up from the causeway to the beach. The April breeze carried the scent of confederate jasmine and sweet viburnum tinged with car-exhaust fumes. The town had more visitors than you could stir with a stick, and half of them were young, horny and slightly inebriated. I recalled reading a complaint the British had made about American troops during World War II:

overpaid, oversexed and over here. Apply that to these college kids and you had spring break in Pelican Bay in a nutshell.

Darcy returned, opened the door to my office and stood aside for Jolene to enter.

With luxuriant long brown hair, huge Italian sunglasses, and a tall, gaunt figure, the result of either good genes or semistarvation, the woman was a dead ringer for the late Jackie O. The cut and quality of her linen slacks, cashmere sweater and matching sandals would have made my sister, a world-class shopper, drool.

Darcy gestured to a leather club chair in front of my desk and, once Jolene was seated, asked if she wanted coffee.

The actress shook her head, and Darcy, looking as if she'd give her eyeteeth to stay and hear the woman's story, reluctantly withdrew.

"I'm Maggie Skerritt. What brings you here, Ms. Jernigan?"

"The Internet."

I swallowed my disappointment. If she needed cyber-snooping, she'd come to the wrong place. I was as technophobic as they came and had to hire a computer specialist in Clearwater to do my Web surfing.

"I need a private eye," she continued, "and your firm is the closest one listed on the Web." Her voice was low and husky, as if she'd been crying.

"Why do you need an investigator?" I'd get to the harder questions later.

She drew a deep shuddering breath. "My baby's been kidnapped."

"Your baby?" Recently turned forty-nine, I was no spring chicken, and Jolene had at least fifteen years on me. For her, childbearing age had to be a dim, distant memory. But she'd said *baby*, so maybe she'd adopted.

"Roger." She muffled a sob and fumbled in her purse for a tissue. "He's only three."

Now she had my complete attention. "Have you notified the authorities?"

Her head snapped up, and I could feel the intensity of her gaze behind her dark glasses. "Are you crazy? And have it splashed all over the news?"

"Were you threatened?"

"Huh?"

"Did the kidnappers say they'd harm your baby if you went to the police?"

She shook her head. "No, I just don't want the bad publicity."

Jolene Jernigan was either the dumbest woman I'd ever met or I'd missed something. Or both. "Do you have any idea who might have taken your child?"

"Who said anything about a child? Roger's my dog, an adorable pug."

Bingo. The missing link. "How long has Roger been gone?"

"Since shortly after I had it out with that snotty little bitch." She forced her words through clenched teeth, and her well-manicured nails dug into the expensive leather of her purse.

Snotty little bitch. "Another dog?"

"Of course not." She yanked off her sunglasses and glared at me with red-rimmed eyes. Her perfectly plucked eyebrows lifted in an expression of perpetual surprise, and her skin stretched taut as a drumhead across her cheekbones, the obvious result of repeated cosmetic surgeries. Only the crepe lines on her neck gave away her age.

I dug deep for patience. "With whom did you have it out?"

"Grace Lattimore. She's been my personal assistant for the past thirty years."

"Why don't you start at the beginning, Ms. Jernigan, and tell me exactly what happened?"

Jolene rammed her sunglasses atop her dark hair, devoid of any hint of gray. She crossed her legs, bounced one foot like a metronome and leaned back with a sigh. "We arrived at my condo on the beach Friday. My character on *Heartbeats* will be in a coma for the next three weeks, so I finally have some time off."

I made what I hoped were appropriate sympathetic noises and nodded.

"Gracie and Roger always travel with me. And my little precious loves the beach. He was so excited." She frowned. "Unfortunately, when Roger gets excited, he loses control."

I raised my eyebrows, picturing a pug on the rampage but going with the flow in order not to interrupt her narrative with more questions.

Jolene sighed. "He kept piddling on the rugs and furniture. By the end of the weekend, Gracie had her knickers in a twist. 'I was hired as your assistant,' she said, 'not to clean up dog pee.'

"'For as much as I'm paying you,' I reminded her, 'you'll do whatever I ask.' 'If that means cleaning up after that mangy little bugger, I quit,' Gracie screamed. Then she stomped into her room and slammed the door." Jolene smiled and shrugged. "I didn't think too much of it. Gracie quits at least twice a year. Then I give her a raise and she reconsiders. But this time was different."

I nodded. After all that piddle, Gracie, apparently, had reached her limit.

"When I woke up this morning, Gracie was gone, and so was Roger."

"And you think Gracie took him?"

"Who else would have? My condo was locked and the grounds are gated with the tightest security."

Interesting, I thought. As much as Gracie had hated cleaning up after the dog, she'd taken him with her, apparently just to yank Jolene's chain. "Did Gracie leave a note?"

"Nothing. She just left."

"Did she take her belongings?"

Jolene nodded. "And Roger's, too."

I formed a mental image of the pug with a suitcase.

"She took his food and dishes and his box of Milk-Bone treats."

"Sounds as if Gracie at least plans to take good care of him."

Jolene jumped to her feet and paced the recently re-finished hardwood floor. "But he'll miss me. His little heart will be broken," she insisted with all the fervor of an experienced drama queen, before her expression hardened into something ugly. "I want him back."

"Any idea where Gracie might have gone?"

Still pacing, she waved one hand toward the windows. "She has relatives in Largo."

I grabbed a pad and pencil. "I'll need their names and addresses."

Jolene halted in front of the desk and gave me the information. "How soon can you get on this? I really miss Roger."

"I'll start right away." Remembering Darcy's parting instructions, I added, "Of course, there's the small matter of a retainer."

Jolene retrieved her purse from the chair and snapped it open. She extracted a checkbook, wrote a check with a flourish and handed it to me. "This should take care of it. And here's my cell number."

She rattled off the digits, which I scribbled hastily on the pad on my desk.

I rose and walked her to the door. "I'll call as soon as I have something for you."

After Jolene left, Darcy came in. "Did you get her autograph?"

"The best kind."

Darcy's eyes almost bugged out when I showed her the check for $10,000.

Later that morning, after fighting my way through tourist traffic to Pelican Beach, I checked with security at the condo where Jolene owned her penthouse and confirmed that Gracie had indeed departed by cab late Sunday night with Roger in tow. A viewing of the surveillance tape had given me a look at Gracie, who was short, plump and dowdy with cropped straight gray hair and wire-framed glasses. Roger was short, plump, smush-faced and light brown with a black face and ears.

I left the beach and headed to the address in Largo where Gracie's relatives lived. What should have been a straight shot down Fort Harrison Avenue and Clearwater-Largo Road became a rat's maze of work zones and detours. If you're anywhere in Florida during tourist season, you can bet the shortest distance between two points is under construction.

Just south of Bay Drive, Largo's main drag, I found the road where Frank and Ellen Lattimore, Gracie's aunt and uncle, lived. The street's frame bungalows, built in the thirties and forties and shaded by massive live oaks draped in flowing Spanish moss, were small but well maintained, and the lawns were neat and tidy. I pulled onto the crushed-shell driveway of the address Jolene had given me. There was no vehicle in the carport, and with its shades drawn, the house appeared deserted.

On the off chance that Gracie was inside, hiding out, I climbed out of my twelve-year-old Volvo, went up the front walk and knocked on the door to the screened porch. When no one answered, I knocked again, louder, thinking surely Roger, if he was there, would have made some noise.

"They're not home."

At the sound of the loud voice in my ear, I almost jumped out of my skin. I whirled around to find an elderly man standing directly behind me. Dressed in baggy shorts, a sweaty T-shirt and grass-stained sneakers and holding long-handled loppers, he had a short, wiry build and was as brown and wrinkled as a raisin. A battered straw hat covered his head.

"If you're selling something," he said, "or one of those come-to-Jesus people, you're wasting your time."

"You their neighbor?"

"Yup, and you are?"

"Maggie Skerritt. I work for Gracie Lattimore's employer."

His leathery face twisted into a grimace. "The actress."

I nodded. "Have you seen Gracie? I have a message for her."

"You're out of luck. She arrived late last night, but the whole bunch took off early this morning. Even the dog."

"The dog?" At least Gracie hadn't ditched the pooch after she left Jolene's.

"Ugly little mutt. Gracie had it on a lead, and they packed a dog carrier along with the rest of the luggage."

"They were taking a trip?"

"Yup. I promised Frank I'd look after his place while they're gone."

"Did Frank say where they were going?"

The old man shrugged. "Said they were traveling across country to see the sights."

I was good at tracking, but not that good. It's a hell of a big country. "Did he leave a contact number, some way he can be reached?"

"I can give you his cell phone."

"That would help. Thanks."

He turned and walked toward the house next door. I trailed along.

"I hope Gracie knows what she's doing," he said over his shoulder, "dragging her pet along."

"Why is that?"

"Frank hates dogs. Gracie'll be lucky if he doesn't make her leave that mutt on the roadside in the middle of nowhere."

Great, I thought. It looked as if I was going to need the FBI and the SPCA if I intended to find Roger.

After obtaining Frank's phone number, I drove to the nearest shopping center and found a pay phone inside Publix, the grocery store. Bill had been harping at me for years to buy a cell phone, but I hated the idea of everyone being able to reach out and touch me 24/7. For the first time in more than twenty-two years, I was enjoying life without the annoyance of a police radio or a beeper. And, so far, I'd always been able to locate a phone when I needed one.

Locating Frank Lattimore was another matter. Either his cell phone was out of range or he wasn't answering. I hoped I could contact him before he dumped the dog. Although I'd never owned a pet— my meticulous mother wouldn't have one in the house when I was a kid, and, as an adult, I was never home—I loved animals. With his roly-poly body, a gait like a drunken sailor, and a face like an aging prizefighter, Roger was cute in a grotesque way. I didn't want him to end up lost or hurt. But then I've always been a sucker for kids and animals.

By now, it was late afternoon, so I called Darcy. When she reported no messages or other business, I cut her loose from the office and drove toward home, where I intended to spend my evening trying to reach Frank Lattimore.

My stomach was growling with hunger. I'd skipped lunch, knowing every food vendor and res-taurant would be thronged with spring break crowds, creating at least an hour's wait to be served. If Bill hadn't planned to stay overnight in Sarasota, I could have mooched supper off him. He loved to cook and could produce a fantastic meal out of practically thin air in the galley of his cabin cruiser. The *Ten-Ninety-Eight*, named after police radio code for "assignment completed," was where he lived at the Pelican Bay Marina. I, on the other hand, considered my refrigerator stocked if it held a couple of Diet Cokes.

The sun hung low over the waters of St. Joseph's Sound when I pulled into the parking space at my waterfront condo. I tossed my blazer, purse and keys onto the foyer table, removed my gun and holster, kicked off my shoes and crossed the living room to open the sliders that overlooked the water. Fresh, salty air, a perfect complement to the natural wicker and rattan furniture and the blue-green sea colors I'd chosen for paint and fabrics, filled the room. Bill called my decorating style Florida tourist hotel, but I liked the soothing atmosphere. Until my job as a police detective had ended two months ago, I'd spent too little time at home in the twelve years I'd owned the place. Now, working as my own boss, I hoped that would change.

I tried again to reach Frank Lattimore's cell phone with no luck and was headed to my kitchen, hoping supper would miraculously materialize in the refrigerator, when the doorbell rang. I opened the front door to find Bill standing on the front porch.

I don't know which I was happier to see, him with his thick white hair, smiling blue eyes, and deeply tanned physique that would put any college boy to shame, or the two bags of Olive Garden takeout he was holding.

"I thought you were spending the night in Sarasota," I said.

"I missed you. Besides," he said as he hefted the bags, stepped inside and headed for the kitchen, "I knew you'd be hungry."

"You know me too well."

"Not half as well as I intend to."

"What if you discover I only love you because you feed me?"

"Then I'll know how to guarantee your affection for the rest of my life." His grin was devilish. "And you'll gain a hundred pounds."

"Only if you brought tiramisu."

"I did."

"I think I'll marry you."

"I'm counting on it." He unloaded the bags and was transferring food into dishes from the cupboards. "Want to eat on the patio?"

I nodded and picked up a couple of plates and some silverware to carry outside. "Too bad I don't have any wine."

"I thought of that, too." He pulled a bottle of Chianti from one of the bags. "Can't have Italian food without a good red wine."

"You sure you don't have an ulterior motive?" I asked.

"Of course I do. I drove back from Sarasota because I don't want to sleep alone."

I grinned. "The food alone would have worked. The wine is overkill."

"Better to have it and not need it—"

"Than to need it and not have it." I finished one of his favorite sayings for him.

Later, sated with linguine and too much wine, I leaned back in my chair and watched the sun drop toward the horizon. I told Bill about our newest case, Jolene Jernigan and the missing Roger.

"Frank Lattimore's not answering his cell phone," I said, "so, at this point, I'm stumped."

Bill swirled the last of the wine in his glass. "It doesn't make sense that Frank, who doesn't like dogs, would agree to take Roger on a cross-country trip."

"Maybe they dropped off the dog to be boarded," I said. "I'll start calling kennels and vets in the morning."

We watched the sun disappear before Bill spoke again. "Have you talked with your mother lately?"

"You sure know how to throw cold water on a perfect evening."

"I take it that's a no?"

"You take it right."

My eighty-two-year-old mother, with whom I'd never been close, had ostracized me from the family circle before Christmas last year when I'd arrested the daughter of her best friend during a murder investigation. Although I'd eventually managed to clear the woman and find the real killer, Mother was still miffed. She hadn't even thanked me for her Christmas present, a gaffe that my socially correct parent would commit only under the direst of circumstances.

"You have to make the first move," Bill said.

"I've *been* moving. I sent her a Christmas gift,

and I've called several times. But Estelle—" Mother's housekeeper "—always says that Mother is out or asleep or unavailable."

"Priscilla's not getting any younger. You'd better mend your fences while you can."

"I would if I knew how. Mother's never liked me, and I haven't a clue why." The shrinks would have a field day with me, pushing fifty and still at odds with my mother. "She never approved of my career in law enforcement, but her dislike started long before that. Even as a child, I relied on Daddy to run interference between us. I wish Daddy were alive now."

"Try sending flowers."

I considered his suggestion. "A few dozen roses and crawling from here to her place on my bare knees might do the trick."

"Just don't wait too long," Bill warned.

He spoke from experience. His only surviving parent, his father, resided in an Alzheimer's facility in Tampa, and hadn't recognized Bill for the past few months.

"Can we talk about something cheerful?" I asked.

"How about dessert?"

"Great. Tiramisu always makes me smile."

Bill gathered dishes to carry inside. "I'll have to hit the sack soon. I want to get up early to beat rush-hour traffic when I return to Sarasota."

My tiramisu smile widened. Good food, great wine, my favorite dessert and early to bed with the man I loved. It didn't get any better than that.

CHAPTER 2

With both the dog and my dognapping suspect in the wind, I was back at the office early Tuesday morning, calling boarding kennels and polishing off a double vanilla latte and a fresh cruller from the bookstore coffee shop downstairs, when Dave Adler sauntered in.

Adler had been my partner before the Pelican Bay Police Department went belly-up, and I'd developed a maternal attachment to the bright young guy. I considered him the son I'd never had and also held a special affection for his wife Sharon and daughter Jessica, an adorable toddler fast approaching the terrible twos. Ironically, I felt closer to the Adlers than to my own family.

"What happened?" I asked. "The Clearwater PD finally give you a day off?"

This was his first visit to our new office, and he was glancing with interest around the spacious, high-ceilinged room with its tall windows that over-looked downtown with its quaint shops, the marina and the waters of Pelican Bay. "Nice digs, Maggie. How's the P.I. business?"

I shrugged. "Bill and I are staying busy. He's working background checks in Sarasota this week. He'll be sorry he missed you. How's the job treating you?"

His confident, cocky attitude faded, and his handsome face sobered. "I need your help."

"You got it."

"We found a DOA at Crest Lake Park before dawn this morning, shot sometime last night with a small-caliber gun."

The mere mention of murder made my skin itch. "You've worked your share of homicides. Why do you need me?"

He pulled at his earlobe, barely visible beneath his shaggy sandy hair, and scowled. "There were only two items found in her purse besides her driver's license and wallet. The first was a slip of paper with your name and address on it."

My skin irritation increased as I wondered

whether I'd known his victim. Probably just a prospective client, I assured myself, not someone I actually knew. "What was her name?"

"Deirdre Fisk."

"My God." I sank back in my chair and struggled to catch my breath. "I haven't heard that name in sixteen years."

Memories assaulted me, images of pale, bloated bodies on the medical examiner's table, young girls not yet in their teens, who'd been sexually abused, strangled and dumped into Tampa Bay.

"How did you know her?" Adler folded his tall frame into the chair across from my desk and waited.

I took a sip of coffee. "Deirdre Fisk was the lucky one."

"Not last night."

"Remember the cases I told you about, the child murders Bill and I worked more than sixteen years ago when we were partners on the Tampa PD?"

Adler nodded.

"Deirdre Fisk was only nine years old then. She was abducted by the man we assumed was our killer and taken to a mangrove on the Tampa causeway. She probably would have been murdered like the other three victims, except a couple of guys fishing a few yards offshore heard her screams. They started the motor on their boat and headed for the beach. At their approach, her abductor shoved her out of his vehicle and took off."

"Did she ID him?"

I shook my head. "You know how kids are. She described him as an old man, which could have meant anybody over twenty. And driving a big white car. She didn't know the make or model. The fishermen saw only taillights as the man made his escape."

"So the guy was never caught?"

"The close call either scared him off—unlikely, since sexual predators can't control their impulses— or, more likely, he moved away, or was arrested and imprisoned for some other crime, or died. Whatever the reason, the child killings stopped, and Bill and I never caught our perp."

Adler pointed to the hives I was scratching on my forearms. "That's when those started?"

"My allergy to murder?" I nodded. "That's also when I left the Tampa PD and moved home to Pelican Bay. I thought working at the department here would cut down on my homicide cases."

Adler's laugh held no warmth. "You sure got that wrong."

Before the Pelican Bay Department had been disbanded and local policing had been assumed by the county sheriff's office in February, Adler and I had solved four murders in as many months.

"Now I'm chasing dognappers," I said. "Much less pressure."

But I couldn't help remembering the scared little girl with silvery blond hair and big blue eyes, who had shivered with shock and terror while I questioned her about the monster who'd abducted her. And now she was dead. "Tell me about Deirdre Fisk."

"Not much to tell," Adler said. "That's why I'm here."

"Her family moved out of state after her ordeal. What was she doing back in the Bay area?"

Adler reached into his jacket pocket, extracted an evidence bag and slid it across the desk. "That's the other item we found in her purse."

I picked up the bag and read a recent newspaper clipping from the *Tribune* through the plastic. The article documented the presentation of a special scholarship to a Tampa teen by Florida's governor. Accompanying the text was a photograph of the boy and his parents with the governor and, behind them, several other adults, whom the caption identified as members of the Florida legislature, including Juanita Menendez from Tampa, Ronald Warner from Bradenton, Carlton Branigan from Clearwater, and Edward Raleigh from Pelican Bay.

"Maybe Deirdre knew the teen or his family," I suggested.

"It's possible. But, according to the victim's driver's license, she lived in Pennsylvania."

"That's where the family moved after they left Tampa. Have you notified next-of-kin?"

Adler nodded. "Her parents are deceased. Her only living relative is an older sister Elaine, who moved back to Tampa a few years ago. I just came from her apartment, where Deirdre's been visiting the past two weeks."

"Did the sister say why Deirdre had my address and this news clipping?" I asked.

"That's what I'm trying to find out, but Elaine's not cooperating."

"You think the sister's involved?"

Adler shrugged. "Hard to tell. She didn't want to talk to me about Deirdre's business."

"So why come to me?"

"The entire department's covered up with spring break," Adler said. "We're all working double shifts, dealing with traffic, drunk and disorderlies, and other minor infractions. Since you already have a connection with the family, I'd really appreciate your interviewing the sister. See if you can find out what Deirdre was doing on this side of the bay in Crest Lake Park in the middle of the night."

"You got it. When's the autopsy?"

"Tomorrow morning at ten. Want to observe?"

The Tampa children's murders had haunted my dreams and frustrated my waking hours for years. Getting involved with Adler's homicide case would either put my nightmares to rest or stir them up again. My love/hate relationship with police work and my obsession to catch a killer who'd eluded me for too many years won out.

"I'll be there. It'll be good to see Doc Cline again."

Adler stood to leave. He paused at the doorway and circled his face with his finger. "Get your Benadryl refilled. From the looks of the splotches on your face, you're going to need it."

* * *

As soon as Adler left, I asked Darcy to complete the calls to local kennels and vets in search of Roger, and I headed for Tampa.

Driving across the Courtney Campbell Causeway that spanned Tampa Bay, I passed four locations etched in my memory. Three of the spots were boat ramps where a young girl's body had been brought ashore. The fourth was where the fishermen had discovered nine-year-old Deirdre Fisk, naked, freezing and traumatized.

Unlike those dark, tragic nights that I shuddered to recall, the road today was drenched with light. Towering oleanders, bursting with white and pink blossoms and shimmering in the brilliant sun, lined the causeway. Vehicles bearing out-of-state license plates jammed every lane. Most cars were overflowing with young people, luggage and coolers, and many sported surfboards, boogie boards, beach umbrellas and folding chairs strapped to the roofs. Everyone seemed bound for a beach and in no particular hurry to get there.

By the time I reached Elaine Fisk's apartment complex in Temple Terrace, it was after eleven, but

I doubted the woman had reported for work on the day her sister had been murdered.

I parked in a visitor space, climbed the stairs to Elaine's second-floor apartment and rang the bell.

No one answered, but I could hear sound from either a television or radio inside.

I rang the bell again. "Elaine? It's Maggie Skerritt. Will you talk to me?"

Someone switched off the sound inside, and a moment later, the door opened a crack with the chain still on. I pushed my ID through the opening.

"I'm sorry to bother you at a time like this, but I need to talk to you about Deirdre."

The door closed. I heard the chain unhook, then the door opened again. Elaine Fisk blinked in the sunlight, her eyes the same pale blue as her sister's, her hair the exact silvery blond, but uncombed and tangled. About thirty years of age, she was dressed in gray sweatpants and a Hard Rock Hotel and Casino T-shirt. Her feet were bare, and her face was swollen from crying.

"Come in." She stepped aside, and I entered her living room.

The draperies were drawn and no lights were on. My eyes took a moment to adjust to the gloom. The apartment was filled with dark, heavy furniture, the kind many newcomers bring south from Northern homes and that doesn't mesh with Florida's bright sunshine and oppressive heat. A few knickknacks, porcelain statues and framed pictures cluttered the tabletops. Elaine motioned me to a sofa, turned on a lamp, and curled into a chair across from the couch.

"I'm sorry for your loss," I said. "Detective Adler told me about Deirdre."

Elaine, her eyes glazed with shock, nodded.

I glanced around the dreary room. "Is there anyone you can call to be with you?"

She hunched her shoulders. "Deirdre was all the family I had. My friend Katy's working, but she'll try to get off early this afternoon and come over."

I hoped Katy could make it.

"I'm helping Detective Adler investigate Deirdre's murder. Can you tell me why she was back in Tampa?"

Elaine gazed past me, her eyes unfocused. "She came to visit me. If she liked the area and it didn't bring back the nightmares she had as a kid, she was planning to move so—" she swallowed hard "—so we could be together. Deirdre was lonely living in the big house in Pittsburgh after Mom and Dad died."

"Why was she in Clearwater late last night?"

Elaine curled deeper into her chair and avoided my eyes. "I promised Deirdre I wouldn't tell anyone."

I took a full breath and spoke in my gentlest voice. "The only connection I had with Deirdre was when I investigated her abduction here in Tampa all those years ago. Was that why she wanted to see me?"

Elaine's lower lip trembled. "I warned her not to stir things up again."

"Is that why she was coming to see me?" I repeated. "About that case?"

She hesitated, then nodded. "But only if she was sure."

"Sure of what?"

"That the man in the newspaper picture was the man who tried to kill her."

"The picture in the clipping she was carrying from the *Tribune*?"

Elaine nodded again.

"Which man?" I asked.

She shook her head and twisted a lock of hair around one finger.

"I know you promised Deirdre not to talk about it, but you may hold the key to solving her murder."

She appeared to consider my claim before finally saying, "Deirdre wouldn't identify which man. She didn't want to accuse anyone falsely. She said she had to see the man first and be certain it was him before she came to you with her suspicions."

Deirdre's body had been found in a park less than five miles from my office. Had she identified her assailant and been on her way to tell me? Or was she headed to Branigan's house in Clearwater or Raleigh's home in Pelican Bay and had met with foul play unrelated to the man in the newspaper photo?

"I'm sorry I can't be more help," Elaine said.

"There is one way you can. Do you have a recent picture of Deirdre I can borrow?"

Elaine removed a photograph from a frame on the table beside her and handed it to me.

I slid the photo into the pocket of my blazer. "I don't know who killed your sister, but if it was the man who abducted her as a child, and if he thinks you might know about him, you could be in danger, too. Maybe you should move in with Katy for a while, until we get a better handle on what happened to Deirdre."

She shrugged, apparently too numb with grief to feel fear. "I'll see. When will they let me have her? I want to take her back to Pennsylvania and bury her beside my parents."

"Detective Adler will let you know." I took a business card from my pocket and handed it to her. "In the meantime, if you remember anything else or if you need me, give me a call."

I stood to leave. Elaine remained huddled in her chair.

"Lock the door after me," I said. "And don't let anyone in you don't know."

An hour and a half later, I sat at the pass-through counter between my kitchen and dining room and ate leftover linguine for a late lunch. Then I called Adler to tell him what I'd learned from Elaine Fisk.

"Thanks," he said. "You had better luck with her than I did."

"I guess she trusted me because Deirdre trusted me. So what's your next move?"

"I'll track down Ronald Warner in Bradenton and the father of the scholarship winner. You think you could interview Branigan and Raleigh to find out where they were last night?"

"Sure, but who's going to interview the governor? He was in the picture, too."

Silence filled the other end of the line before Adler finally spoke. "You're kidding, right?"

"Most politicians are guilty of something." But I didn't really believe the governor had been involved in Deirdre's murder. If Deirdre had been looking for him, she'd have gone to Tallahassee, not Clearwater. "The governor's a high-profile guy who's been in the national spotlight for years. If he'd been her abductor, Deirdre, despite living in Pennsylvania, would have noticed television footage and newspaper pictures of him long before now. But even so, it wouldn't hurt to determine his whereabouts at the time of the original murders."

"I'll get on it. Thanks for your help, Maggie."

"No need to thank me. This is one case I've been wanting to crack for years."

I broke the connection, then dialed the office. Darcy answered and informed me that she'd struck out on vets and kennels. No one had any pugs boarded, so Gracie wasn't hiding Roger under an assumed name.

Jolene was not going to be happy with my lack of progress, but I owed her an update. Luckily, only voice mail answered on her cell phone, so I didn't have to deal with her disappointment. I left a message, telling her what I'd discovered so far and that I'd be in touch.

With a Diet Coke in hand and the portable phone tucked under my arm, I pulled that indispensable investigative tool, the telephone directory, from a kitchen drawer and went out to the patio. My intention was to call every Lattimore in the book to see if Gracie had other relatives who could be taking care of Roger. But at the sight of thirty-five Lattimores listed in Upper Pinellas alone, I changed tactics.

Twenty minutes later, I was knocking on the door of Frank Lattimore's neighbor in Largo. The Raisin answered, dressed much as he'd been the day before in grass-stained work clothes sans hat. His bald head was as brown as the rest of him. Many Florida retirees live for their yards, and, unless they hire a lawn service, in a climate that's either too hot, too cold, too wet, too dry, and with soil that's basically nutrient-poor sand, keeping a landscape green and well trimmed can be a full-time job.

"Now what?" he asked as soon as he recognized me.

I love a man who gets straight to the point. "Does Frank Lattimore have any relatives in the area, someone to contact in case there's a problem with his property?"

"You still looking for Gracie?"

I nodded. "Frank's not answering his cell phone."

"He never does. He's on one of those bare-bones calling plans. Only uses the danged thing for emergencies."

"What if you have to get in touch with him?"

"He checks in with me every so often."

"Have you heard from him since he left yesterday?"

The Raisin shook his head. "But you might ask Slim."

"Slim?"

"Frank's brother-in-law. Lives two blocks over." He jerked his thumb toward the south.

"Why didn't you tell me this yesterday?"

"You didn't ask."

He had a point. "What's Slim's address?"

The Raisin rattled off the street and number and shut the door.

The drive to Slim's house, an almost identical twin to his brother-in-law's, took only a couple of minutes. As soon as I left my car and slammed the door, I knew I'd hit pay dirt. Inside the house, a dog was barking and throwing himself at the front door. When I rang the bell, the barking escalated, and the thuds against the door grew more violent.

"Roger, is that you?" I said.

For a moment, the noise ceased, as if the dog had recognized his name. Then the uproar continued, more fierce and frantic than before.

A woman's voice cut through the hullabaloo. "Roger, stop that! Bad dog!"

Roger gave one last bark, as if to show who was really in charge, and silence fell.

"Who is it?" a woman asked.

"Maggie Skerritt."

"What do you want?"

She didn't open the door, and I didn't blame her. Most women I knew didn't open their doors to strangers, even in daylight.

"I'm looking for Gracie Lattimore."

"Why?"

"Jolene Jernigan sent me."

"Jolene can go to hell."

"Are you Gracie?"

"Doesn't matter if I am. I'm not talking to you."

"You don't have to," I said in my most conciliatory voice. "Just give me Roger so I can take him home."

"No way. I want her to suffer, just like she's made me suffer all these years, the ungrateful hag."

"She could call the police, press charges. Then you'll be in a heap of trouble."

"Ha! Fat chance. She's too paranoid about bad publicity. At her age, she's only inches from being canned by the producers. She causes them any problems, she's history."

Jolene didn't need a private eye. She needed a hostage negotiator. I'd give it my best shot. "What can I do to help resolve your differences?"

Gracie's reply was an anatomical impossibility, so I tried again. "C'mon, Gracie. Jolene says Roger piddles when he's upset. He's probably missing Jolene now, and you don't want him ruining your relatives' carpets."

"Roger's happy as a clam," the disembodied voice behind the door said. "He never liked Jolene anyway."

"Surely there's something Jolene can do to get him back?" I was growing hoarse from shouting through the door.

"Yeah, she could apologize for treating me like dirt, but hell will freeze over first."

"You know how it is working for someone else." I remembered my days with Chief Shelton, who'd made my life miserable at every possible turn. "Sometimes you're the windshield, but most days you're the bug. That's life. If you want warm and fuzzy—"

"Get a dog? That's exactly what I did."

"I was going to say go into business for yourself."

"Yeah, right. I've got thirty years' experience as a doormat. What business could I go into?"

I was more concerned about the dog. "You won't hurt Roger?"

Her reply rang with outrage. "What kind of a person hurts a helpless animal?"

Too many that I'd met in my line of work. "Will you be staying here, so I can contact you in case I can come up with a solution?"

"Where else would I go? Thanks to Ms. High-and-Mighty, I don't have a home of my own."

I considered my options, but they were limited. If nothing else, I could stake out the house and grab Roger when Gracie took him for a walk, but she didn't sound like the type who'd give him up without a fight. I decided to work on the apology angle with Jolene first.

"I'll be in touch. And if you change your mind, here's my card with my number."

I slid the card through the mail slot in the front door. Firm jaws and strong teeth snatched it out of my hand. Roger's, I assumed, but then I didn't know that much about Gracie.

I'd have to pass near Carlton Branigan's neighborhood on my way back to Pelican Bay, so I detoured into Harbor Oaks in Clearwater to question the state senator for Adler. Basically, I needed only to determine the man's whereabouts the night Deirdre was killed. If he didn't have an alibi, Adler would do the follow-up interview.

The tree-lined streets of the historical district were filled with homes from the same era as the Lattimore house, but all similarities stopped with the vintage. These residences in Harbor Oaks were stately mansions on acres of landscaped yards, not unlike the house where I'd grown up in Pelican Bay and where my mother still lived.

The Branigan residence resembled an English Tudor country mansion, complete with ivy-covered walls, mullioned windows, and a bronze stag with a full rack of antlers, standing guard on the sweeping front lawn. The Anglican effect extended to the tall butler with ramrod posture who answered the front door.

"May I speak with Senator Branigan, please?" I handed the man my business card.

"The senator isn't in." His snooty British accent fit the decor. He took my card and held it between his thumb and index finger as if it were contaminated.

"Is Mrs. Branigan in?" I said.

He looked annoyed. "Come in, and I'll check."

I stepped into a dim but impressive two-story foyer that showcased the soaring ceiling, timber framing, and a broad staircase that rose to a gallery across the back of the house.

"Have a seat." The butler indicated a massive carved chair with a high back and velvet upholstery that looked like a throne, then walked toward a door at the rear of the foyer. His careful tread made no sound on the thick Oriental carpet.

I settled into the chair and looked around. Through a broad arch across the foyer, I could see straight through to the living room. Although the lighting there was also dim, a recessed ceiling fixture above the mantel threw a wash of illumination over a life-size portrait of a man in his mid-thirties with fair hair and a ruddy complexion. Dressed in an expensive three-piece suit, he sat in a chair similar to the one I now occupied and held an open book on his lap. His other hand rested on the head of a large dog, some kind of wolfhound. The man in the portrait was a younger version of the Carlton Branigan in Deirdre's news clipping.

Surveying the elegant surroundings, I concluded that Branigan, who'd worked in city, county or state government as long as I could remember, certainly hadn't suffered financially from being a public servant. That fact jostled a memory, a tidbit gleaned from my mother's love of gossip. Carlton Branigan had married money. His wife's family had owned most of downtown Clearwater and the southern half of Clearwater Beach at one time. Without the clout of official police credentials, I doubted the influential woman would agree to see me.

But I'd promised Adler, and I wouldn't leave without determining where Branigan had been last night. With a sigh of resignation, I decided to play a card I usually kept well hidden in the deck.

"Excuse me," I called to the butler as his hand reached for the doorknob.

He turned. "Yes?"

I imitated the tight, condescending smile I'd seen my mother use too many times. "Tell Mrs. Branigan that I'm Priscilla Skerritt's daughter."

CHAPTER 3

Wealth has its privileges, and apparently invoking Mother's name had provided access to Stella Branigan. The butler returned quickly, and I followed him through the rear hall onto a wide flag-stone terrace that ran the width of the back of the house. Broad stairs swept down to formal gardens and a swimming pool. Past the pool, a long arbor, covered in confederate jasmine thick with blossoms, led to a tennis court. Clearwater Harbor glistened beyond the seawall in the late-afternoon sun.

The elegant ambience made me uncomfortable until I remembered a saying I'd read somewhere that the upper crust is a bunch of crumbs held together by dough. In my former life as a librarian, I'd done a great deal of reading. But that was before my fiancé, a doctor in residence, had been murdered by a crack addict in the emergency room, and, as a result, I'd entered the police academy, determined to spend my life fighting crime. Working in law enforcement hadn't left much time for reading. And between Deirdre Fisk and Jolene Jernigan, I was too busy now as a private investigator to indulge in my favorite pastime.

On the south end of the terrace, an older woman sitting at a glass-topped wrought-iron table looked up at our approach.

"Bring us tea, Madison," she said in a low, cultured voice that rang with authority.

"Yes, ma'am."

Madison returned to the house, and Stella Branigan waved me into a chair opposite her. "You're Margaret Skerritt?"

"Yes."

"I know your mother. We served together on the Art Guild board."

She crossed her legs, leaned back in her chair and lit a cigarette with a gold lighter. In her early sixties, tall and athletic with big bones and a long, horsey face, Stella Branigan would have been homely under other circumstances, but excellent makeup, a salon haircut and well-fitted casual clothes provided the illusion of attractiveness.

"How is Priscilla?" she asked.

"Mother's fine. Still active."

"But you're not here to talk about your mother." Her smile barely lifted the corners of her mouth.

"No. I'm helping the Clearwater Police Department with one of their investigations."

She was still for a moment, and her carefully composed expression gave nothing away. She exhaled cigarette smoke. "We don't have much crime in Harbor Oaks. Good security systems, Neighborhood Watch, and excellent policing deter most criminals."

Footsteps on the terrace stairs below interrupted her. A thirty-something man, dressed in tennis whites and with a face like Stella's but Carlton's fair hair and ruddy coloring bounded up the steps. He stopped abruptly when he spotted me.

"Sorry, Mother, I didn't know you had company. I came to invite you to have dinner with us."

"It's not a problem, darling. Ms. Skerritt will be leaving soon. Margaret, this is my son, Sidney. He lives next door."

Sidney stepped forward and shook my hand. "I'll wait inside until you're finished here."

"No need," his mother said. "Our conversation isn't private."

He pulled out a chair and joined us at the table.

"It's really your husband I need to speak with," I said to Stella.

Stella shook her head. "Carlton's in Tallahassee. He won't be home until late tonight."

"Was he here for the weekend?"

"No, he stayed at the Capitol for a fund-raiser last night. Now he's taking care of loose ends at his office before coming home for the spring recess. Is there something I can help you with?"

I reached into my pocket and withdrew the photo of Deirdre Fisk. "Have you ever seen this young woman?"

I gave Stella the picture. She glanced at it, and a brief flicker that could have been no more than interest rippled across her angular features. But her facial expression was bland again when she handed the photo back.

"I've never seen her," she said in a disinterested tone.

"May I see?" Sidney asked.

His mother seemed annoyed when I passed him the photo. He looked, but returned it without comment.

"Ms. Fisk didn't come here looking for the senator last night?"

Stella stiffened. "What are you implying?"

"I'm not implying anything. Just trying to help the Clearwater Police establish a time line on this woman's whereabouts."

"What makes you think she'd come here?" Sidney asked.

"She had a newspaper clipping in her purse with a picture that included the senator. We think she might have been trying to contact the men in the photograph."

Sidney frowned. "Why?"

"She may have known one of them when she was a child," I hedged. No need to bother Stella further. I'd double-check Carlton's alibi, but, if he was in Tallahassee last night as his wife claimed, he couldn't have killed Deirdre Fisk.

Madison appeared with a silver tea service, but I'd learned all I needed to know. I pushed to my feet. "I won't take any more of your time. Thanks, Mrs. Branigan. Nice to meet you, Sidney."

Sidney smiled somewhat distractedly. Judging from the impatience in his body language, I figured he was in a hurry to discuss something with his mother.

"I'm sorry I couldn't help you more," Stella said. "Madison, please show Ms. Skerritt out."

I followed the butler to the front door, then stopped and took out the photo of Deirdre. "Has this woman been here lately?"

Madison gazed at the picture and shook his head. "Mrs. Branigan only recently returned from Tallahassee."

"When exactly was that?"

"I am not allowed to talk about my employers, a condition in my contract."

"Thanks." For nothing.

He shut the massive wooden door behind me, and I walked to my car.

The Clearwater Police Department was only minutes away. I arrived to find Adler working late. He was at his desk in CID and eating a foot-long steak-and-onion hoagey. Rarely had I seen Adler when he wasn't eating, but where he packed the calories on his lean, muscular body was a secret many would kill for.

"Branigan's wife claims he was at a fund-raiser in Tallahassee last night," I said.

Adler wiped grease from his fingers and turned to his keyboard. With a few strokes, he accessed the Internet and pulled up a Tallahassee newspaper Web site. A few more keystrokes, and a news photo of Branigan and the governor, taken at Monday night's party, appeared on his monitor.

"The wife's story checks out," he said. "You talked to Edward Raleigh yet?"

"Next stop," I said. "What have you got?"

"According to this photo with Branigan, the governor was in Tallahassee Monday night, too. But I did some digging before you got here, and your Tampa murders occurred during his first run for office."

"The one he didn't win?"

"Right. But his publicity people released an itinerary for his appearances during that time. It's in the archives on his campaign Web site. I cross-checked it with the dates of the original murders, and the governor was either in South Florida or the Panhandle when all three murders—and the attempt on young Deirdre Fisk—occurred."

I nodded. "He was never high on the suspect list and eliminating him narrows our field."

"The field's getting smaller fast. Ralph Porter, my partner, tracked down the father of the teen who won the scholarship. He was in Gainesville with his son last night, scoping out the campus for the fall semester. The Hampton Inn confirms that the family checked in Sunday afternoon and are still registered."

"And Representative Warner in Bradenton?"

"He wasn't answering his home phone, so I called his Manatee office. His aide says the entire Warner family flew from Tallahassee to Big Sky, Montana, Friday for spring break. Gave me the name of their resort. I reached the manager by phone and he corroborates that they're booked through next weekend."

"So neither of us had any luck."

"How about with your dognapper?" Adler took another huge bite of his sandwich. He must have seen the longing in my eyes. "Want some? I can give you half."

"No, thanks." I was still doing penance for tiramisu and would be counting calories the next few days. "I found the dog, but my client's former employee is holding it hostage."

"That's easy enough. Have a uniform pick up the little beast."

I shook my head. "My client insists on strict secrecy and no publicity. I'll have to come up with another angle. Any ideas?"

"You could always send in Malcolm, disguised as Animal Control." He grinned.

"Maybe, as a last resort."

"By the way, I got a call this afternoon from Elaine Fisk to give me her temporary address and phone number. She said you suggested she move in with her friend for the time being, and she followed your advice."

"Good. If whoever killed Deirdre did so to cover up three other murders, he'll have nothing to lose by taking Elaine out, too, especially if he's afraid she might ID him. But with all but one of our suspects from the photo with alibis, it's looking more likely that her murder was random." I nodded toward the case file on his desk. "Do you have any suspects from the park where Deirdre was found?"

Adler shrugged. "It's a known hangout for drug users and dealers, hookers and homeless. A lot of those vagrants are mentally unstable. Deirdre's wallet was empty. She could have been killed for a few bucks."

"Or the killer could have taken her money to make it look that way."

"We've canvassed most of the known regulars at the park," Adler said. "Either nobody saw anything or nobody's talking."

"Any prints on the wallet?"

"Some smudged partials," he said. "No matches in AFIS."

I considered Adler's description of the park's seedy inhabitants. "There's another possibility. Whoever killed Deirdre could have left her purse untouched, and someone else took her money before the cops came."

The nerve endings in my skin went into spasms, and I reached into my purse for Benadryl caplets.

"The water fountain's over there," Adler said.

I crossed the room, washed down the pills and returned to his desk.

"So—" he dumped the papers from his takeout into the trash "—looks like we've narrowed our news photo suspects to Representative Raleigh."

"Yeah," I said, trying not to scratch, "if you don't count the druggies, vagrants and prostitutes."

"Let's be optimistic. Maybe when you talk to Raleigh tonight, he'll confess and save us a lot of trouble."

I shook my head. "You know what they say."

"What?"

"An optimist claims we live in the best possible world, and the pessimist fears it's true."

He grinned. "You've been at the books again."

"Not often enough. I'll see you at the autopsy in the morning."

Afraid that once I reached home, I wouldn't drag myself out again, I decided to ignore my grumbling stomach and visit Edward Raleigh before I called it a night.

When he wasn't in Tallahassee, Raleigh lived on the edge of the golf course at the Osprey Country Club just north of town. I turned off Alternate U.S. 19 into the entrance of the classy subdivision, drove past the clubhouse that bordered Osprey Lake, and wound my way through the curving streets that followed the configuration of the golf course.

With my car windows down, I caught a faint whiff

of orange blossoms from trees in the spacious yards. The hundreds of thousands of acres of commercial groves that used to overwhelm the county each spring with their heavy perfume were a thing of the past, victims of population growth and development, and the elusive scent made me nostalgic.

The sun was setting when I arrived at Raleigh's sprawling Key West style home, and lights blazed through the angled Bermuda shutters on the front windows. A Cadillac with its trunk open was parked in the driveway, and a middle-aged man and woman stood at the rear of the car, holding pieces of luggage. I couldn't tell if they were leaving or arriving.

I parked in front of the house, and they set down their bags when I left my car and approached them. "Mr. and Mrs. Raleigh?"

"Yes?" the man said.

I showed my ID, clearly legible in the light above the garage door. "I'm Maggie Skerritt."

"I know you," Mrs. Raleigh said. "You're the detective who solved the Lovelace murder back before Christmas."

"I was a detective. Now I'm a private investigator, and I'm helping the Clearwater Police Department with a case."

"We can talk inside," Raleigh said with warm hospitality and a politician's smile. He probably figured me for a registered voter. "We've just returned from a trip to Mobile to visit our grandkids. Our grandson's first birthday was yesterday. It was quite a celebration."

"When did you leave Mobile?" I asked.

"Early this morning," Mrs. Raleigh said. "We drove straight through."

"If you can verify that, I won't take any more of your time."

Raleigh reached into the pocket of his shirt and handed me a slip of paper. "Here's a credit card receipt for gas when I filled up this morning before we left."

The service station's address, time, and date stamp supported his claim. I handed him back his receipt. "Thanks for your help."

"What's this about?" his wife asked.

"Just trying to establish a time line on a woman who was searching for a man in a newspaper photo. Your husband was among them, but, if she came here, you obviously weren't at home."

I thanked the Raleighs for their time, got into my car and headed home. Apparently, Deirdre hadn't been killed by any of the men in the photograph. But that didn't mean that none of them was a suspect in my cold case from Tampa. Tomorrow I'd start digging into old records to see if I could connect one of the men in the photo with the murders I literally itched to solve.

When I arrived home, the message light on my answering machine was blinking. Hoping it was Bill announcing he'd finished his Sarasota assignment and was back on board the *Ten-Ninety-Eight*, I pushed Play.

Instead of Bill's deep voice, I heard Caroline's frantic plea. "Meet me at the hospital. Mother's had a stroke."

CHAPTER 4

Pelican Bay Hospital was only a couple of miles from my condo, close to the former police department, now a county sheriff's substation. During the entire drive, Bill's recent warning about reconciliation rang in my ears, and I worried that I'd waited too long to mend fences with my mother. If she died before I could speak with her, I would never have the chance to bridge the gap between us. I'd long ago accepted that I didn't really like my mother, and I'd also given up on gaining her approval, but I loved her, and I hoped I had a chance to tell her so.

I broke a few traffic laws between my place and the hospital, only to waste endless minutes circling acres of parking lots looking for an empty space.

After finally securing a spot on the far edge of a lot, I sprinted toward the emergency entrance. Nearing the building, I met Joe Fenton, a paramedic, who was leaving, and we spoke in passing.

"Hey, Maggie. Long time no see."

"Hi, Joe," I said without slowing my stride.

"You can tell it's spring break." He smoothed his mustache, which reminded me of a caterpillar. "Just had a drunken college kid take a header off a balcony at the beach."

"Will he make it?"

Joe shrugged. "You know head injuries. Got another call. Gotta run. Good to see ya."

Joe swung into the driver's seat of the ambulance parked at the curb, and I rushed up the brick walkway to the E.R. entrance. The hospital doors slid open with a pneumatic hiss, and I hurried to the waiting room. I'd no sooner stepped inside than an unkempt woman in a floral patio dress and flip-flops threw herself at me. After extricating myself from her viselike embrace, I was surprised to discover that, instead of a Signal Twenty awaiting admission to the psych ward, the distraught and disheveled greeter was my sister. Her informal clothes, uncombed hair and face devoid of makeup made her appear much older than her fifty-seven years and underscored the seriousness of Mother's condition.

"I came as soon as I got your message," I said. "How is she?"

"She's being evaluated now."

"What happened?" I led Caroline to a corner of the waiting room less populated than the others and sat on a vinyl-covered sofa beside her.

My usually cool-as-a-cucumber sister wrung her hands. "A little before eight, Estelle went up the bedroom to tell Mother her dinner was ready."

I nodded. A stickler for propriety, Mother always dressed for dinner and ate in the dining room, even when she dined alone.

"Mother was slumped in her chair, incoherent, unable to move her right arm or leg. Estelle called the paramedics, then me. I got here just as they were bringing Mother in."

I glanced around the motley assortment of humanity that crowded the waiting room. An elderly couple held hands and watched CNN on the ceiling-mounted television. A young mother and father attempted to comfort a red-faced baby who was crying at the top of his lungs, and two teenage girls took turns talking and giggling on the courtesy phone in the corner opposite us. A man in work clothes sat stoically and cradled his arm, as if it was broken.

"Where's Hunt?" I asked.

Caroline seldom went anywhere without her wealthy, socially connected husband, Huntington Yarborough, mother's ideal, obsequious-to-a-fault son-in-law.

"Hunt's in Palm Beach at a securities seminar. I talked with him right after I called you. He's taking the first plane home."

Recent events, mainly Hunt's help in my last murder investigation and his and Caroline's support after Mother disowned me, had me reassessing my relationship with my sister and her husband. We weren't at the warm-and-fuzzy stage yet, but I no longer ground my teeth in their presence.

"Have you talked to a doctor?"

Caroline shook her head. "There's been no time."

"I haven't seen much of Mother lately." That was the understatement of the century. I hadn't seen her at all since she'd laid into me after Thanksgiving for arresting Samantha Lovelace for her husband's murder. "Has she been feeling all right?"

"You know how Mother is. She doesn't talk about illness, as if it's a social taboo. Funny, don't you think, for somebody who was married to a doctor for so many years?"

I nodded. Mother had a long list of social taboos, most of which I'd broken at one time or another.

A nurse at the admitting desk called Caroline's name, and my sister hurried to the counter. While she filled in forms attached to a clipboard, I considered calling Bill on his cell phone, but decided to wait until we'd heard from the doctor. Mother's episode could have been a transient ischemic attack—one wasn't a cardiologist's daughter without picking up some of the lingo—or something much more serious. I'd wait until I knew the diagnosis before bothering Bill.

After what seemed hours but was only about twenty minutes, a young female doctor in pale blue scrubs came out of the emergency room and spoke to the nurse at the reception desk. The nurse pointed her toward Caroline, and I hurried over to hear what the doctor was saying.

"Margaret, this is Dr. Quessenberry," Caroline said. "She's treating Mother."

Dr. Quessenberry smiled and looked about fourteen. Irrationally, I wished for Dr. Fellows. Seton Fellows, my father's best friend, had been an eminent neurologist in his day, but I comforted myself with the probability that this girl was more up-to-date on the latest treatments than a man who'd been retired for a decade.

"How is she?" I asked.

"We've done a CT scan that shows your mother has suffered an ischemic stroke. We're moving her to ICU and administering antithrombotics to dissolve the clot."

"Can we see her?" Caroline asked.

"Just for a moment, after she's settled," the doctor said, "but you mustn't upset her. She needs calm and rest."

Don't upset her. That left me out. I didn't want to precipitate another stroke or aggravate this one.

"You go, Caroline," I said. "I'll wait here."

I returned to the chair in the corner of the waiting room, and Caroline followed the doctor into the E.R. CNN was broadcasting a hot pursuit on a California freeway. The driver was taunting police by sticking his bare behind out the window. Wondering how he maintained control of the vehicle with his fanny in the breeze, I watched to see if he had a passenger who was handling the steering while the driver mooned the cameras.

"Hello, Margaret."

I glanced up to find Seton Fellows smiling down at me from his extraordinary height of six foot five, as if my thoughts had conjured him from thin air.

"What are you doing here?" I asked.

The retired neurologist folded his lanky body into the chair beside me and took my hand. "Estelle called and told me what happened. I came to check on Priscilla."

"Have you spoken with Dr. Quessenberry?"

He nodded. "And Dr. Katz will be taking over in ICU. He's good. I trained him myself."

"Is Mother going to be all right?"

"It takes about ten days before we know for certain that a stroke patient is stable. But the swiftness with which Estelle called for help definitely is a positive factor in your mother's prognosis."

"I'd like to see her, but Dr. Quessenberry says she shouldn't be upset."

He cocked his head to one side. "Why would you upset her?"

I was horrified to find my eyes filling with tears. Decades ago at the police academy, I'd learned never to let 'em see you cry. Tears don't help, and, if nothing else, they rust your gun. I sniffed loudly and took a deep breath to forestall a sob. "She doesn't approve of me. Never has."

With a scowl, he ordered, "Come with me."

He lifted me by the elbow and steered me toward an interior hallway, stopping at the desk on his way out. "If there's any news on Priscilla Skerritt, page me in the cafeteria," he told the receptionist.

"Yes, Dr. Fellows."

"Rank," he whispered to me, "still has its privileges."

We followed the winding corridor and its broad colored-coded stripes on the freshly waxed vinyl floors through the belly of the building to the staff cafeteria. With old-fashioned gallantry, Seton pulled out a chair for me at a wall table in the nearly deserted dining room, then strode to the serving buffet. He returned a minute later with a tray that held two cups of coffee and two slices of pie.

"They make a delicious custard pie." He took the seat next to me. "Comfort food."

I thanked him but didn't think I could swallow anything past the knot in my throat. "You think Mother will be okay?" I asked again, needing reassurance.

"Time will tell. Her constitution is strong, and Priscilla is a fighter, but she is eighty-two, after all."

And I was pushing fifty and feeling like a child, sitting next to Daddy's old friend, who'd bounced me on his knee when I was a toddler. If Daddy couldn't be there, Seton was the next best thing.

"Why doesn't Mother like me?" I asked.

His smile multiplied the wrinkles in his kindly face. "You've always been something of a rebel, Margaret."

"Her dislike goes deeper than my rebellion. I toed the line for Mother for the first twenty-two years of my life, until after Greg was murdered, but from my earliest memories, I sensed a distance between us, a coolness on her part that I've never understood."

Seton sighed and stirred sugar in his coffee. "It's a long story."

"If you'll tell it while we wait, maybe it will take my mind off worrying."

He paused for a moment, as if contemplating what to say. "Just bear in mind that what I'm telling you is only from my personal perspective. I'm a neurologist, after all, not a psychologist."

"Okay. I'm listening." I dumped three packets of sugar in my coffee and tried to warm my cold hands on the foam cup. Hospitals were always cold, as if in hopes the frigid temperatures would somehow thwart death.

"Did you know that your father and Nancy were once engaged to be married?"

"Your Nancy?" Seton's wife of over fifty years had died last spring.

Seton nodded.

"I never knew that."

"It's ancient history, something we never talked about, your father and I, but it's a fact your mother never forgot."

"What happened? I mean, why didn't Daddy marry Nancy?"

"Because of me."

"But you were his best friend."

"That's how I met Nancy, at a fraternity party in Gainesville when Philip and I were both undergraduates. We couldn't help it, Nancy and I. Even though she was engaged to your father, we fell deeply in love. We explained it to Phil, and he understood."

"Did she break his heart?"

"He wasn't happy about it. He and Nancy had grown up together here in Pelican Bay. Their families were close, and almost from infancy, everyone had assumed that they would marry. I believe Phil was in love with Nancy, but she said she hadn't known real love until she met me."

The story was beginning to sound like a script for Jolene Jernigan's *Heartbeats*, but it was a facet of my parents' life I'd never known, and I was fascinated.

"So where did Mother come in?"

"The following year, your father proposed to Priscilla. Like Margaret, Priscilla was a local girl he'd known all his life."

"Did he love her?"

"Not at first."

"Then why did he marry her?"

Seton smiled. "Because in those days, that's what people did. Men had their careers, women kept the home fires burning, had children, and supported their husbands in their endeavors."

"Did Mother know he didn't love her?"

"She was always jealous of Nancy," he said with a nod, "but she shouldn't have been."

"Why not?"

"Because by the time you were born, your father had grown to love Priscilla deeply. She was a delightful companion, a superlative hostess, a boon to his practice. He worshipped the ground she walked on."

"And they lived happily ever after?"

Seton frowned and shook his head. "I wish I could say so, but there was always a cloud hanging over their marriage."

"Me?"

"Good Lord, no, Margaret. You were your father's darling...but that was part of Priscilla's problem."

"I don't understand."

"And I'm not sure I can explain it properly. You see, your mother, for all her bluff and bluster, is a very insecure woman. She was never able to let go of the fact that she had been Philip's second choice, not even after he'd learned to love her more than he'd ever loved Nancy."

"But what's that got to do with her feelings about me?"

"She could see the way your father adored you, totally and unconditionally. We all saw it. But her inferiority complex kept her from realizing that Phil adored her the same way."

"She resented me?"

His smile was gentle. "Not you. She resented that you received what she wanted desperately, your father's love."

"But you say she had it."

"There are none so blind as those who will not see."

"So she projected her jealousy of Nancy onto me?"

Seton nodded and sipped his tepid coffee. "Unfortunately for you. But she'd deny that fact with every fiber of her being if you confronted her with it, because she won't allow herself to face it."

That my mother had resented my father's affection for me cut like a knife, but it also explained her attitude, the distance and disapproval that, until now, I'd never understood but had felt personally responsible for.

"Did Daddy know?"

"He sensed your mother's discontent, but he was never able to convince her that she came first in his life."

"Because she kept pushing him away?"

His gray eyebrows shot up in surprise. "You knew that?"

I shrugged. "Mother keeps everyone at arm's length."

"She's afraid of being hurt, of not measuring up," Seton said.

"Of not being Nancy?"

He nodded. "The irony is that Philip loved your mother more than he ever loved Nancy."

"And the tragedy is that Mother never knew." I tried a bite of the custard and had to wash it down with a swallow of coffee. "Where's the TV Dr. Phil when you need him?"

Seton finished his pie and patted his lips with his napkin. "If you look back over all the ways you rebelled, going into police work, refusing to marry and raise a family, those acts were salt in your mother's wounds. Priscilla, who had conformed in every possible way to her picture of the perfect spouse, never felt Philip's approval, while her errant daughter had her father's unquestioned affection. She became a bitter woman where you're concerned."

"Why tell me this now?"

"Your mother's an old woman. Even if she survives this stroke, her time is limited. I'd hoped that age would give her wisdom, but Priscilla has never recognized her insecurities, so she can't let them go. I don't want you going through the rest of your life thinking there was something you could have done or said that would have changed her. There isn't. This is Priscilla's problem, one I fear she'll never come to grips with."

Seton had turned my view of my mother on its head. I'd always considered her strong, impervious to life's vagaries, in control. I'd never guessed that her self-confident facade was a cover-up for self-doubt.

I sighed. "She always approved of Caroline."

"She had to," Seton said. "Caroline is an extension of herself. If she didn't affirm Caroline, she'd be rejecting the life she'd chosen for herself."

"Has Mother ever been happy?"

Seton shrugged his bony shoulders. "That's a question I can't answer except with another. Can people who aren't honest with themselves be happy?"

I felt an overwhelming sadness for Mother and the life she'd never lived, the happiness she'd never known. I prayed harder than ever that she'd survive this stroke and that her close call would give her insight, make her examine her past more closely. And, selfishly, that then she'd be able to love me.

"More coffee?" Seton asked.

I shook my head.

"Then let's go see how your mother's faring."

CHAPTER 5

After returning from the cafeteria and saying goodbye to Seton, I called Bill from the waiting room courtesy phone, told him about Mother's stroke and that, according to both her doctor and Caroline, she was resting comfortably.

"I can be there in an hour and a half," he said.

"I'll be okay," I assured him. "Will you finish in Sarasota tomorrow?"

"I should be back in Pelican Bay by dinnertime, unless you need me sooner."

How much I needed him scared me, but I wasn't about to admit it. "I'll keep you informed."

"I love you, Margaret."

I glanced at the sea of faces in the waiting room,

as many watching me as CNN. "Back at you," I said, and hung up.

Outside of ICU, I spoke with Caroline again. Hunt was on his way to the hospital from the airport, Mother was still resting comfortably, and I was feeling about as useful as a chaperone at a bachelor party. When Caroline insisted there was no reason for both of us to stay, I didn't argue.

Rather than return to my lonely condo after leaving the hospital, I drove to Mother's house, a Mediterranean-style mansion designed by Misner in the twenties, that sat on two acres of waterfront property. I parked out front and took the path around back to the kitchen entrance. The entire house was dark when I knocked on the door.

"Estelle, it's me, Maggie."

Estelle, who'd been with Mother since before I was born, lived in a suite of rooms off the kitchen. I knocked again, and light spilled from the kitchen windows. Locks rattled on the kitchen door, it swung open, and I was smothered in the embrace of the woman who'd been more of a mother to me than my own. As always, Estelle's scent of Ivory soap triggered memories of happy times and unconditional acceptance.

"Miss Margaret, bless your heart. What you doing here?" Her ebony face, unwrinkled despite her seventy years, glowed with pleasure, and her delight in seeing me warmed my heart.

"I came to give you a report on Mother."

Estelle drew her terry-cloth robe tighter around her ample curves and tightened the sash. "Miss Caroline done called from the hospital just a few minutes ago."

"Then I'll let you go back to bed."

"You do no such thing. I haven't laid eyes on you since Thanksgiving. You think I'm gonna let you walk out now without sitting down for a visit?"

Unlike Mother, Estelle was never too tired or too busy to be bothered by me. I slid onto the chair at the big kitchen table where I'd sat every afternoon after school, regaling Estelle with my childhood woes and accomplishments. Except for new appliances, the kitchen, with its old-fashioned glass-faced white wooden cabinets, black-and-white floor tiles in a checker pattern, and high windows that flooded the room with sunshine during the day, hadn't changed.

"You had your dinner?" Estelle asked.

"Yes," I lied, even though my leftover linguine lunch was a distant memory. She'd ply me with food otherwise, and I had no appetite.

Estelle eased onto a chair opposite me at the table and folded her hands, gnarled with arthritis, on the tabletop. "I hear you gonna marry your Mr. Malcolm."

I nodded. "Next February. Valentine's Day."

If I didn't get cold feet and chicken out. Bill had proposed Christmas Eve and suggested a long engagement to give me time to get used to the idea of marriage before taking the plunge. Not that I didn't want to marry him, but I feared ruining a decades' old friendship. Bill claimed that friendship made the best foundation for marriage, and I was staking our future on the hope that he was right.

"I'll mark that date on my calendar," Estelle said, "'cause I been waiting a long time to bake your wedding cake. I'm happy for you, child. You been alone too long."

"Look who's talking."

Estelle appeared surprised. "I'm not alone. I've always had you and Miss Caroline and Miz Skerritt."

Skepticism raised its head. I knew what a tyrant Mother could be. "Is Mother good to you?"

"She treats me fine. Even helped put my nephew Tyrone through medical school."

"I never knew that."

Estelle shrugged. "Miz Skerritt don't talk much about her business."

"She hasn't talked much to me about anything."

Estelle reached across the table and patted my hand. "Miz Skerritt keep to herself. In lots of ways, she's not real sure of herself."

Bill had tagged my mother as insecure the first time he met her. I'd brushed his assessment off as an erroneous first impression. After my talk with Dr. Fellows, I knew better.

I squeezed Estelle's hand and leaned back in my chair. "How come everybody knew about Mother's insecurities but me?"

"'Cause she's your mama, honey. Hard to see anything past that."

Estelle was right. Mother had always loomed large and invincible in my life. I found it hard to believe she was lying helpless in a hospital room.

"Have you thought," I asked, "about what you'll do when she comes home? You'll need to move her bedroom downstairs, hire more help—"

Estelle laughed. "I won't have to do diddly. I 'magine Miss Caroline will take care of everything. You know how she is."

"A force of nature."

"Like her mama. I just go with the flow."

I glanced at the clock over the sink and shoved to my feet. "It's late. I'd better go. You'll call me if you need me?"

Estelle nodded and enveloped me in another hug that made me feel less like an orphan than I had when I arrived.

Caroline's morning call at seven o'clock to inform me that Mother had spent a peaceful night and was regaining some mobility on her right side had yanked me out of a sound sleep. I rolled over, punched my pillow and pulled the covers over my head, but I couldn't go back to sleep. My to-do list for the day, topped by contacting Jolene Jernigan and attending Deirdre Fisk's autopsy, kept scrolling through my brain.

I flung the covers back and headed for the shower.

In my office an hour later, bolstered by coffee and glazed doughnuts from the bookstore coffee shop, which mercifully opened early for the downtown breakfast crowd, I sat at my desk and stared at a photocopy of the newspaper article from Deirdre Fisk's purse.

Was one of those men the worst kind of killer, a sexual predator who murdered children? Or had one of them simply borne an unfortunate resemblance to the man who'd abducted Deirdre more than sixteen years ago?

Only one thing was certain. Deirdre wasn't talking.

I quickly ruled out the governor. Not only was he basically a good man—for a politician. He'd lived too long in the public spotlight. Hiding such a dark secret would have been almost impossible with the kind of scrutiny he'd endured, especially from his political enemies. Any hint of dirt on him or his family had been unearthed and aired long ago.

I made a list of the names and addresses of the other four men in the photo, then reached for the phone. First I called the florist and ordered a bouquet of spring flowers to be delivered to Mother at the hospital.

Then I punched in the number for Jolene's cell. Her sleepy and irritated "What?" when she answered told me I'd awakened her.

"Sorry to call so early, but I've found Roger."

"Damn, you're good." Her husky voice came from a throat that had inhaled too much cigarette smoke.

She sounded so pleased I hated to burst her bubble. "Not that good. Gracie won't give him up. She wants an apology first."

Her sigh of exasperation resonated in my ear. "Then tell her I'm sorry and pick up the dog."

"She wants more than a simple apology."

"Like what?"

Like if you die, she'll forgive you. If you don't, she'll see. "I have no idea. Maybe a significant raise, a personal letter asking forgiveness, some kind of extravagant gift."

"Grovel and take her back? Under those circumstances, she'd make my life hell."

I sighed. Gracie was the bug, and Jolene definitely wanted to be the windshield. "Then your only other option is to call the police."

"No cops. No publicity. You think of something. That's what I'm paying you for." She broke the connection.

I was beginning to understand how Gracie felt and was sorry Jolene didn't have another dog I could kidnap. But wishful thinking wouldn't get Roger back. Maybe Adler's suggestion of Bill's impersonating Animal Control wasn't so bad after all. As I left for the medical examiner's office, I decided to run the idea by Bill when he returned from Sarasota.

The April morning was another chamber of commerce winner: brilliant blue skies, warm temperatures and a fresh salt-laden breeze. Looking at Deirdre Fisk's pale body on the stainless-steel autopsy table in the Medical Examiner's Largo complex, I couldn't help thinking of the hundreds of thousands of young people without a care in the world currently thronging the Florida beaches. Deirdre, on the other hand, in her short lifetime had suffered more than any human should ever have to bear.

Doris Cline, the medical examiner, dressed in green scrubs and a clear plastic face mask that reminded me of space travelers in old sci-fi movies, worked with efficiency and an effervescent cheerfulness that belied the grimness of the setting.

"It's good to see you again, Maggie." With a digital camera, she snapped pictures of the body from every angle with all the enthusiasm of a wedding photographer. "When the Pelican Bay PD folded and you retired, I was sure you'd never witness another of my autopsies."

"This homicide may be related to some cold cases," I said, "ones Malcolm and I had in Tampa in the late eighties."

"That's why I asked Maggie to be here," Adler said.

He stood on the other side of the table, breathing through his mouth, hugging a barf bucket and swallowing hard. Despite his macho appearance, he had a tough time at autopsies. Some cops eventually learned to disconnect from the horror of the procedure; others never did. I suspected Adler fit in the latter group.

"No defensive wounds," Doc said as she continued her examination. "Nothing beneath her nails to indicate a struggle. Appears our victim either knew the shooter or was taken completely by surprise."

With her thick gray hair, tan and fit body and boundless energy, Doc reminded me of a perennial cheerleader. How she maintained her upbeat attitude amidst all this death and decay mystified me. She had to be a special breed.

"The victim was in a public park in a strange city after dark," I said. "You'd think she'd have been on alert under those circumstances."

"Unless she recognized the person she came to meet," Adler said.

I nodded. "But that would rule out druggies and vagrants as suspects."

With deft work with her scalpel and a wicked-looking electric saw, Doc opened the thorax and removed and weighed organs. The relentless hum of the air-conditioning and the noise of Doc's instruments were the only sounds in the cold, tiled room, awash in the glare of overhead lights. Adler held up okay until Doc applied the saw to the victim's skull. Then his barf bucket came in handy.

"Attend enough of these," I said to him with a sympathetic smile, "and you'll eventually make it all the way through without hurling."

He shook his head and wiped his mouth with a paper towel from the dispenser beside the sink. "I hope to God I don't ever get used to this."

Doc was examining the brain. She probed and removed a bullet, dropped it into a metal tray and handed it to Adler.

"Looks like a .22," he said. "I'll have ballistics run it, see if they have a match."

"So," I said, thinking out loud, "from the looks of the angle of entry and the powder burns on the underside of her jaw, the victim was approached from the front, the gun pressed beneath her chin and fired upward into her brain before she had time to react."

Doc nodded. "She died instantly."

I looked at Adler. "And nobody heard the shot?"

"The spot where the body was found isn't far from Gulf-to-Bay Boulevard, six lanes of continuous heavy traffic, even at night, especially during spring break. If someone did hear the gunshot, it might have sounded like a car backfiring."

"No sign of sexual assault," Doc said. "You said she was robbed?"

Adler nodded. "Her wallet was empty, but, according to her sister, she didn't have much cash."

Doc shrugged. "Then it could have been simply a case of wrong place, wrong time."

I wasn't buying that scenario. "She didn't run, didn't fight. The shot was up close and personal. She knew her killer."

Adler's cell phone rang, a simple chime, not one of those canned polkas or tinny renditions of "The Battle Hymn of the Republic" that drove everyone within hearing nuts. He stepped into the adjacent room to take the call.

Doc was stitching the Y-incision and glanced up at me. "How's this victim related to your cold cases?"

"Remember the young girls murdered and dumped in Tampa Bay in the late eighties?"

Doc nodded. "I know the Hillsborough M.E. who performed those autopsies. You grow a thick skin in this business, but all those children—there's no skin thick enough for that not to get to you."

"Deirdre here was the only little girl who escaped. Her sister says that before Deirdre was killed, she had come to this side of the bay to try to ID the man who abducted her all those years ago."

"You think she found him?" Doc asked.

"Not according to the info we have."

"Maybe he found her."

Adler stepped back into the room. "Maggie, want to ride with me?"

"What's up?" I asked.

"Another homicide."

Doc cursed beneath her breath. "If there's one thing I hate, it's keeping busy."

"Who was killed?" I asked.

"State Senator Carlton Branigan. He's been murdered in his own backyard."

CHAPTER 6

Clearwater Police cruisers and a paramedics van filled the circular driveway in front of the Branigans' Tudor-style residence. Adler parked behind the van. Ralph Porter, his current partner, met us out front, and Adler handled the introductions.

"The Fisk murder is related to some cold cases of Maggie's from her days on the Tampa PD," Adler explained. "Fisk was found with a photo that included Branigan, so Maggie's got a dog in this fight."

Tall and gangly, Porter was dressed in stiff new jeans, a red-checkered shirt and a string tie. His sandy hair was combed in the pompadour style favored by used-car salesmen, television preachers and Elvis impersonators. With a wide grin splitting his long face, Porter reminded me of Gomer Pyle—but with brains.

"You think Branigan's connected to Fisk?" His drawl matched his hayseed appearance.

"So far only by that picture in the vic's purse," Adler said. "Where's the body?"

"This way."

We followed Porter through the foyer, where a uniformed officer was taking a statement from Madison, the butler, who'd shed his hoity-toity demeanor and looked ready to jump out of his skin. From the corner of my eye, I spotted another uniform sitting with Mrs. Branigan and her son, Sidney, in the living room.

Porter led us out the rear door, across the terrace, down to the lawn, and around the pool to the long arbor that connected the pool deck to the tennis court. A profusion of confederate jasmine thick with tiny white blossoms covered the curved trellis, creating a tunnel of shade in the midday light. The flowers' heavy fragrance didn't completely mask the coppery stench of blood.

Carlton Branigan, dressed in white tennis shorts and shoes and a pastel yellow shirt, lay midway down the path, sprawled facedown on the brick walkway. Tennis rackets, bottles of water, towels and cans of balls spilled from an open carryall beside him.

Adler knelt next to the body. I was only an observer, so I stayed back, hands in the pockets of my blazer, mouth shut.

"This is the first case like this I ever had," Porter said, shaking his head. "The guy was garroted—by a damned vine. Almost took his head off."

A length of jasmine vine, made up of several strands that had grown entwined like a braid, was wrapped around Branigan's neck and had cut deeply into the skin and muscles. Blood oozed around it. The vine had been pulled from the arbor and was still attached to the rest of the plant.

During one of my few forays into gardening, I'd tried to clear errant strands of jasmine from my patio trellis and had found it as strong as piano wire. When I'd called on the condo maintenance man for help, he'd laughed at my frustration. "I told the association when they requested putting in this stuff that it's fast growing and tough. You should plant it with a shovel in one hand and a machete in the other."

The rugged vine on the arbor had made a perfect murder weapon, handy and lethal, which suggested that the murder hadn't been premeditated but a crime of passion. Extreme passion, judging from Branigan's semidecapitated state.

"Doc Cline's on her way," Adler said. "She'll be able to confirm strangulation. From the angle of his head, I doubt his neck's broken."

"Branigan's a big guy," Porter observed. "Would have taken another big guy to do this."

Or rage, I thought. I'd seen small men—and women—perform incredible feats when they were high on adrenaline or drugs.

Adler examined Branigan's hands. They were covered with deep cuts and stained with chlorophyll, as if the victim had tried to pull the vine from his neck during the attack. Aside from the disturbed growth on the trellis, no other sign of a struggle was visible on the hard brick surface of the path. No footprints. No apparent fibers or other visible elements. And the well-covered arbor would have screened the assault from any witnesses.

Footsteps on the path announced the arrival of Doc Cline. She surveyed the area with a quick glance. "Looks like a scene from *The Attack of the Killer Vines*. You guys bring any weed spray?"

Her wisecrack reminded me how much I missed

the gallows humor of police work. Cops had to laugh to keep from screaming all the way to the funny farm.

"I'll stay with Doc," Porter said to Adler. "You take the wife's statement."

Adler nodded. "Maggie, you're with me."

We returned to the house, and Adler dismissed the uniform in the living room.

Mrs. Branigan, dressed in a well-cut tennis dress with a matching cardigan, sat on a chintz-covered sofa, chain-smoking, judging by the overflowing cut-crystal ashtray on the table beside her. Sidney, wearing casual slacks and a golf shirt, paced in front of the massive fireplace below the portrait of his father and ran shaky fingers through his thinning blond hair.

I settled on a window seat just inside the door, and Adler took a chair opposite Stella Branigan.

"I'm sorry for your loss, Mrs. Branigan," he said, "and I'm sorry to bother you at a time like this, but I need you to tell me exactly what happened."

"She already told the other officer." Sidney's stance and tone were belligerent, a role reversal of the young guarding his mother.

"I need to hear it again," Adler said gently. "The sooner we gather the facts, the better our chance of catching your husband's killer."

Stella stubbed out one cigarette and lit another with her gold lighter. She made no effort to conceal the tremor in her hands. "What do you want to know?"

"When did your husband return from Tallahassee?"

"He flew in late last night."

My skin was itching like crazy, and I wished I hadn't left my Benadryl in my car. Branigan's murder was possibly connected to the killings years ago that had precipitated my allergic reaction to homicides, and I intended to find that link. Deirdre Fisk had had a clipping that included Branigan's photo in her purse. Deirdre was dead. Now Branigan was dead, too. And I didn't believe in coincidence.

"When did you last see your husband alive?" Adler asked.

"We had breakfast on the terrace this morning and planned to play tennis." Although her hands shook, her voice was steady. She appeared to be in shock, as if she hadn't totally processed the fact that her husband was dead. "We were finishing our meal when Madison announced that George Ulrich had arrived and demanded to see Carlton."

"George Ulrich?" Adler asked. "The Pelican Bay councilman?"

I felt an irrational surge of hope. Ulrich had been instrumental in shutting down the Pelican Bay Police Department, and Adler and I and every former member of the PBPD would love nothing more than to lock up the guy for murder.

"Ulrich is my father's opponent in the upcoming primary," Sidney said.

Stella shifted in her chair, a move that called attention to her long, tanned legs in amazing shape for a gal in her sixties. Had to be the tennis.

"Carlton told Madison to show George out to the terrace," she said, "and to bring more coffee. I excused myself to go upstairs. I didn't want to interfere in Carlton's business, and I had notes to write and calls to make." Her composure almost cracked but she regained it quickly. "If I'd stayed with him, Carlton might still be alive."

"What happened next?" Adler prodded.

I watched Sidney, watching his mother and hanging on every word. A muscle ticked under his left eye, and he shoved his hands in the pockets of his slacks.

"I was upstairs in my day room that overlooks the terrace," Stella said. "Even though the windows were closed, I could hear Carlton and Ulrich shouting at each other."

"What were they saying?" Adler asked.

Stella shook her head. "I was trying to work, so I blocked out most of it, but what little I heard indicated they were arguing over the campaign."

Adler nodded. "And then?"

"I finished my notes and my calls. Then I went downstairs to find Carlton. When he wasn't on the terrace, I thought he'd gone ahead to the tennis court. I took my racket and walked down to meet him." The color drained from her face, and she took a long pull on her cigarette. "That's when I found him in the arbor."

"How long were you upstairs?" Adler asked.

Stella exhaled a cloud of smoke. "Not more than an hour."

"And your husband and Ulrich argued all that time?"

She closed her eyes, as if trying to recall, then

opened them again. "I don't think so. You can ask Madison what time Ulrich left. He keeps track of such things."

"What did you do after you found your husband?" Adler said.

"I ran back to the house and had Madison call 911. Then I called Sidney. He came right over."

"You were at work?" Adler asked her son.

"In a manner of speaking. I'm in real estate. This morning I was working at home, next door."

"Alone?"

"My wife and daughter are visiting her mother in Sarasota, but my housekeeper has been there since early this morning. You're welcome to talk with her."

Adler jotted in his notebook. "Did you and your father get along?"

Stella gasped, and Sidney's face flushed.

"He was my dad." His face crumpled in grief, and he sobbed, "I loved him."

"Of all the nerve." Stella drew herself straight in her chair and fixed Adler with a haughty stare. "You should be arresting George Ulrich, not questioning Sidney."

Adler opened his mouth as if to speak. I knew he wanted to explain that, statistically, victims are murdered by those closest to them, but apparently he thought better of it, closed his mouth and his notebook, stood, and turned toward the door.

"We'll be in touch, Mrs. Branigan. If you think of anything else, please give me a call."

I started to follow Adler.

"Margaret," Stella said. "Would you stay a moment, please?"

"I'll check with Porter and meet you out front," Adler said, and left the room.

Sidney glanced from his mother to me with a puzzled look. Wondering what Stella Branigan wanted, I was feeling somewhat puzzled myself.

"Yes?" I said.

Stella stubbed out her cigarette. "I want to engage your firm, Pelican Bay Investigations."

"Why?" Sidney blurted before I had the chance.

Stella spoke to him, but her cold blue gaze locked with mine. "I want Ms. Skerritt to investigate your father's murder."

Sidney beat me to the punch again. "The Clearwater Police are already on the case. Why hire a private detective?"

"It's spring break," Stella said. "The police are inundated. I've watched enough television crime dramas to know that the more time that passes, the less likely your father's killer will be caught." She nodded to me. "That's why I want you to start right away. I read in the *Times* about your success in solving the diet clinic killings and the Lovelace murder. Will you work for me?"

I didn't hesitate. I had my own reasons for wanting to solve this case. "You bet. I'll get right on it."

"And you'll report directly to me?" Stella ordered.

"Of course, but I'll have to work with the Clearwater detectives. Otherwise, I won't have access to the forensic evidence."

She nodded. "My husband was a great man. He would have been governor someday. I want his killer to pay for what he's done."

Two things struck me as I walked to meet Adler at his car. One, Stella Branigan hadn't shed a tear during the entire interview. And, two, Darcy was going to kick my butt.

I hadn't asked for a retainer.

CHAPTER 7

"Porter's going to pick up George Ulrich for questioning," Adler said as he drove me back to the M.E.'s office to get my car.

"You think Ulrich's your perp and Branigan's murder was no more than political rivalry gone wrong?" My gut was telling me otherwise, that Branigan's death was somehow tied to Deirdre's.

Adler shook his head. "You taught me well, Maggie. I don't form conclusions this early in an investigation. I just go where the evidence takes me. Besides, the butler said Ulrich left at least half an hour before Mrs. Branigan found the body, leaving time for someone else to have killed Branigan. Then again, Ulrich could have exited through the front door and circled to the backyard to confront Branigan a second time."

"Maybe the butler did it," I suggested. "He's a cold fish if I ever saw one."

Adler shot me a curious glance. "Did Mrs. Branigan tell you anything useful after I left the room?"

"She hired our firm to investigate her husband's murder."

He tightened his grip on the steering wheel. "She doesn't think Clearwater CID's up to the job?"

I felt like a mom reassuring her kid that he'd make the team. "Stella Branigan knows how busy the police are. You already have the Fisk murder to deal with. Besides, Stella is a high-maintenance woman who demands lots of attention and is willing to pay to get it. And I'm happy to take her money."

Adler threw me a grin. "You don't fool me, Maggie. As interested as you are in anything that involves your cold cases and Deirdre Fisk, you'd have worked the Branigan murder for free."

"True. And an added bonus would be to throw Ulrich's conniving political butt in jail." I resisted the urge to rub my hands with glee at the poetic justice of Ulrich being arrested by two former Pelican Bay cops. "What are my chances of watching when you question him?"

"Good—if you promise to share anything you find in your investigation."

"You've got a deal."

We reached the M.E.'s office, and Adler pulled into the parking lot next to my Volvo and called Porter on his cell phone. He listened for a moment, then snapped his phone shut. "Ulrich's wife says he's in a meeting in Lakeland. He's volunteered to come directly to the station for questioning after his meeting ends. Can you meet me there? Ulrich should arrive about two hours from now."

"Wouldn't miss it for the world." I climbed out of the car.

Alder's face split into a boyish grin. "And all on Stella Branigan's tab."

"Hey, lawyers aren't the only ones with billable hours."

Thinking how much I enjoyed working with Adler again, I shut the door and watched him drive away.

I made a quick stop at the hospital on my way back to my office. At the reception desk, an elderly volunteer with silver-blue hair, a candy-stripe pinafore and gracious manners informed me that Mother had been moved from ICU to a private room.

I took the elevator to the third floor, got off and followed the directional signs to 358. I glanced inside before entering. Mother was asleep, and Caroline, reading a hardcover book by Dan Brown, sat in a chair beside the bed. Like Mother, she considered paperbacks common and wouldn't be caught dead with one, despite their portability, their ease on the advancing arthritis in her hands, and the fact that their content was exactly the same as the more expensive editions.

In addition to having picked up reading material, my sister looked as if she'd just come from a beauty spa. Her bottle-blond hair was perfectly styled, her subtle makeup perfection. Unlike the rumpled patio dress she'd worn last night, today she was decked out in a lavender skirt and twin set with color-coordinated Prada heels. I knew the brand because Prada was what she claimed she always wore. The only shoes I called by name were Mary Janes and Buster Browns, echoes from my childhood. I bought shoes that didn't hurt my feet or cost a fortune, and I couldn't care less what their names were. For that reason and several other fashion transgressions, Caroline considered me a barbarian.

A string of pearls and matching earrings completed Caroline's flawless outfit, which had to be brand-new. I'd never seen my sister in the same clothes twice. As for me, it was a good thing clothes didn't come with an expiration date. Otherwise I wouldn't be able to wear anything in my closet.

When Caroline looked up and saw me hovering in the hall, she closed her book and stepped out of the room.

"How is she?" I asked.

"Making remarkable progress. Dr. Katz said he's never seen anyone recover so quickly. She's hoping to go home in a few days."

"That's good."

I was relieved, but, recalling what Dr. Fellows had told me earlier, I also felt a wave of anger at the woman who had denied me the acceptance and affection I'd craved all my life. Guilt followed hard on anger's heels. How could I be mad at an old woman who'd just suffered a stroke?

I gazed past her sleeping form to a flower arrangement the size of a small refrigerator that filled the top of the table beside her bed. "I see she got my flowers."

Caroline redirected my gaze to the windowsill and a porcelain teacup, filled with miniature jonquils and hyacinths. The refrigerator bouquet, I assumed, had come from Caroline and Hunt. My sister always managed to outdo any gift I gave my mother.

"Your flowers are very sweet," Caroline said. "Mother was pleased."

"Really? I haven't been her favorite person lately." *Make that ever.*

"I know." Caroline patted my shoulder in a rare display of sisterly affection. "But I think this episode has her rethinking her attitude."

I could hope, but I wouldn't hold my breath. "I'm working on a case, so I can't stay. Tell her I stopped by."

"Do you need Hunt's help?"

My brother-in-law, the insurance agent, considered detective work exciting and longed to be an amateur sleuth. He had no idea of the long hours of boredom, sitting on surveillance or digging through records. Of course, compared to his rate tables and actuarial charts, watching paint dry would be exciting. "Thanks for the offer, but Bill and I have it covered."

Taking me by surprise, Caroline hugged me. "You're a good kid, Margaret."

Touched, I hugged her back. "Been a long time since either of us was a kid, sis."

I hurried away with only a lingering twinge of guilt at the knowledge that I wanted to escape before Mother awoke.

I swung by the office to check my messages before meeting Adler at the Clearwater PD and was surprised to find Bill already there.

"I finished up in Sarasota as soon as I could, in case you needed me." He enveloped me in a bear hug, then held me at arm's length and studied my face. "You okay?"

"Fine."

"And your mother?"

"She'll probably outlive me." I'd wait till later to tell him what I'd learned from Seton Fellows. "We've been hired by Stella Branigan to investigate her husband's murder."

"I heard about his death on the car radio on the drive back," Bill said. "I'm glad for the work, but why hire us? Isn't that Clearwater's jurisdiction?"

I nodded. "But Stella Branigan strikes me as the kind of woman who likes to be in control. She can't tell the police what to do, so we're it."

"Where do we start?"

"Adler and his partner are interviewing a suspect and said we can observe, but we'll have to hurry. I'll fill you in on the way over."

Bill hugged me again and kissed me hard. "It's great working together, just like old times."

I smiled to myself, still tasting his kiss and thinking, *Just like old times—only better.*

George Ulrich couldn't see Bill and me through the one-way glass in the Clearwater PD interview room where Adler and Porter double-teamed him.

Most suspects are uncomfortable under the harsh glare of fluorescent lights and the intense scrutiny of interrogators, but not Ulrich. Being suspected of murder did nothing to dull his aura of arrogance and self-importance. He'd never made a secret of his political aspirations, which had been his motivating force in helping the sheriff's office take over Pelican Bay policing. In his sixties, with a short Napoleonic figure and thinning hair styled in a comb-over, Ulrich wore a well-tailored blue suit that barely concealed his paunchy stomach, a red power tie and a crisp white shirt.

"I'm a busy man," he complained. "Can we get on with this?"

"We'll ask the questions," Porter shot back, undaunted by the politician's egotism.

"Tell us about your visit to Carlton Branigan this morning," Adler ordered. "His wife and the butler both described you as fired up."

Ulrich took a leisurely swallow from the can of root beer Adler had given him and cleared his throat. "I admit it. I'm mad as hell at Branigan. His flunkies are running a smear campaign against my wife, and I don't like it one bit."

Ulrich had made life hell for the entire Pelican Bay Police Department, destroying their jobs, upending their lives. Now a political enemy had made his life miserable. What goes around, comes around, I thought.

"If he can't beat me on the issues," Ulrich was

saying, "and has to resort to mudslinging, then he doesn't deserve to win. That's what I told him."

"He didn't win," Porter drawled. "No doubt about that."

"Mind if I look at your hands?" Adler asked.

Ulrich seemed puzzled, but he held his hands above the table, palms down. The skin on the back of them was mottled with age spots.

"Turn them over," Adler ordered.

Ulrich flipped his palms upward. Even at a distance, I could tell that they were soft and smooth.

"Those hands didn't strangle Branigan," Bill said in a low voice. "The vines would have scored marks on his palms."

"Unless he wore gloves." I wanted Ulrich to be guilty and was struggling to remain objective. "But if he went to Branigan's to kill him, you'd think he'd have taken a weapon. Especially since Branigan had almost a foot of height and fifty or sixty pounds advantage."

"Maybe he didn't plan to kill him," Bill said, "but when Branigan wouldn't agree to back off Ulrich's wife, Ulrich killed him in a rage."

"Then we're back to the unmarked hands." As

much as I longed to charge Ulrich, my instincts were telling me he wasn't our killer.

We watched Adler and Porter ply Ulrich with questions, which he answered without hesitation.

"He's sticking to his story," Bill said, "and even though he's furious over Branigan's tactics, I don't think he's our man."

Unfortunately, I agreed. Either Ulrich had supernatural control over his body language or he was an innocent man. A self-serving bastard, but not a murderer.

But if Ulrich hadn't killed the senator, who had?

Unable to shake his story, Adler and Porter finally cut Ulrich loose. I thanked them for letting us observe, and Bill and I walked to his car in the station parking lot.

Twenty minutes later, we were sitting in our favorite booth at the Dock of the Bay, watching the sun set over the marina. Primarily a family restaurant but with an adjacent active and noisy bar, the place was packed with tourists. On the ancient Wurlitzer jukebox, Alan Jackson and Jimmy Buffett were belting out, "It's Five O'Clock Somewhere," and most of the crowd in the bar were singing along.

While sipping beer and waiting for our order, I filled Bill in on everything I knew about the Fisk murder and my conversations with Stella Branigan.

"So how do you think we should approach our investigation?" I asked.

Bill considered for a moment, drawing circles with his finger in the condensation on his beer mug. "Tomorrow I'll check with Branigan's political aides and see if any enemies other than Ulrich turn up. You can go to Tampa."

I nodded. "To follow the Fisk connection."

"Study the cold case files at the PD and see if anything jumps out at you."

"I'll also have another chat with Elaine Fisk."

Bill raised his eyebrows.

"She might know more than she's let on," I explained. "Suppose, despite her insistence to the contrary, that Deirdre had told Elaine that Branigan was the man who had tried to kill her sixteen years ago. Elaine would hold him responsible not only for that attack but also for the fact that Deirdre was murdered while trying to hunt him down. That's a pretty powerful motive."

Bill nodded. "Elaine could have confronted Branigan and killed him."

"It's a stretch, because Elaine's a small woman, but rage sometimes provides superhuman strength." Bill and I had worked enough homicides to know that every angle, however unlikely, had to be pursued and eliminated.

Our meal arrived, honest-to-God hamburgers with all the trimmings on homemade buns and the best French fries in the Bay area. Real artery-clogging delights that we allowed ourselves only occasionally. Bill took a big bite, chewed with gusto and swallowed. I dipped a fry in ketchup.

"What about Roger?" he asked.

"Damn." In all the excitement over Branigan's murder, I'd forgotten about the dog.

I related my latest conversation with Jolene and her insistence that we come up with a plan. Bill nixed impersonating Animal Control.

"Maybe we should use part of Jolene's retainer and buy the dog back," he suggested.

"Offer Gracie five thousand dollars?"

He nodded. "We'd be five thousand richer and case closed."

"It might work," I said. "We'd have Roger, but Gracie would be out of a job."

"It won't hurt to try," he said with a shrug.

"You or me?"

He dug into his pocket for a quarter. "We'll flip for it."

I lost the toss, so I planned to stop by to see Gracie before heading to Tampa tomorrow.

We finished our meal and walked back to the *Ten-Ninety-Eight*.

10-98. Assignment completed. I no longer worked for the police department, but I would never consider my assignment in law enforcement finished until the monster who had killed those little girls was arrested and convicted. My gut was telling me that my old nemesis was somehow connected to the murders of Deirdre Fisk and Carlton Branigan. And my skin was itching like hell.

Bill steadied me as I climbed on board. Inside the cabin, I settled on the loveseat in the lounge. Bill sat beside me and turned on the radio to a station playing "The Music of Our Lives."

"We need to talk, Margaret."

"Isn't that what we've been doing?"

"We're getting married in ten months. We have to make plans."

"What's to plan? We agreed on a small civil ceremony."

He wrapped one arm around my shoulders and pulled me close. "I know you don't want to live on the *Ten-Ninety-Eight*, but your condo's only a one-bedroom, a tight squeeze for the two of us. We should decide where we want to live."

The thought of moving, of upsetting the comfortable status quo I'd enjoyed the past three years since Bill had retired, bought his boat and sailed back into my life, sent my nerve endings into fresh spasms.

"We shouldn't rush into anything," I said.

"Rush?" Bill laughed. "I've been wanting to marry you for twenty years. We haven't exactly hurried up to this point."

Call me a stick-in-the-mud, but I'd always hated change. And the older I grew, the less I liked alterations and transitions that disturbed my comfortable rut. I'd lived in my condo more than twelve years. It had been the one constant in my chaotic lifestyle, and I was having trouble visualizing living anywhere else.

"You know how tight the real estate market is," Bill said. "Pinellas is the most densely populated county in the state, and more people are moving here in droves every day. And property values are escalating through the roof. If we want to find the right spot, we should start looking now."

"We're in the middle of a murder investigation," I protested, hoping to delay the inevitable. "Where will we find time to meet with real-estate agents?"

He tugged me closer and tucked my head beneath his chin. His voice rumbled in his chest beneath my ear. "We work for ourselves now. We take the time whenever we want."

Bill could be stubborn. He was determined to find a home for us, and tonight, tired and frustrated by the recent murders, I found it easier to go along.

"What kind of place do you have in mind?" I said.

I couldn't see myself living in a subdivision. At my age, I was well past the soccer-mom stage, and neither Bill nor I liked lawn work.

Bill shrugged. "No preconceptions. Why don't

we just see what's out there? It'll be fun, like a treasure hunt."

More like a root canal. I envied his boundless optimism, his joy in living, and wished it would rub off on me. He seemed to have some kind of internal switch that allowed him to turn off all thoughts of work, to compartmentalize his job from the rest of his life and release his inner child to play. Maybe it was a guy thing.

I should be so lucky. Later, lying in his arms in the wide berth in the cabin, rocked by the waves, I couldn't get the pictures of little girls' bloated bodies out of my mind.

CHAPTER 8

The sun was rising when I left the *Ten-Ninety-Eight* the next morning. I wanted an early start, in case I was lucky enough to snag Roger and had to detour back to the beach to return him to Jolene before heading for Tampa.

Most party-hearty tourists were still asleep, and the marina was deserted and quiet, except for the raucous cries of gulls scavenging for breakfast. The wind was calm, and not a single ripple disturbed the glassy surface of St. Joseph Sound, where a light mist rose from waters cooler than the air.

I returned to my condo for a quick shower and change of clothes and to call Adler for the address of Katy, Elaine Fisk's friend. A second call to the nurses' station at the hospital assured me that

Mother had spent a restful night with no complications.

By eight, I was turning onto the Largo street where Gracie was staying at her Uncle Slim's.

From down the block, I spotted her in her pajamas, robe and bunny slippers, walking Roger on a lead, so I parked a few houses away to keep from spooking her and having her run back inside. As soon as I left my car and locked the door, however, Roger sighted me, gave a joyful yip and dragged Gracie toward me. When he reached me, he stood at my feet, wagging his tail and looking exactly as if he was smiling.

Firmly grasping his leash, Gracie leaned over with her hands on her knees and struggled to catch her breath. "It's okay, he won't bite," she managed to wheeze.

I figured Gracie needed the exercise more than Roger.

"Hey, Rog." I scratched the pug behind his ears. "Good boy."

Gracie snapped to attention when I called Roger by name. "Who are you?"

"Maggie Skerritt. I spoke with you the other day, through the door."

Gracie's eyes widened with a hopeful expression. "Did you bring an apology from Jolene?"

"Not exactly."

Gracie scooped up Roger and clutched him against her chest, as if afraid I'd snatch him away. She narrowed her small eyes behind her glasses. "What exactly?"

"I have an offer. I pay you five thousand dollars, you give me the dog."

"Five thousand dollars?" With her lips puckered in disapproval, she shook her head. The sum wasn't having the effect I'd hoped for. "That's peanuts. Roger's a celebrity dog. I could sell him for more than that on eBay."

Roger, fortunately, had no idea what Gracie was suggesting. Still smiling, he squirmed in her arms, trying to free himself to chase a squirrel digging at the foot of a nearby tree.

"You'd actually do that?" I said with a surge of sympathy for the poor animal that was the rope in this tug-of-war between Gracie and her employer. "You'd put him up for auction?"

Hesitation flickered only for a moment on her

features before Gracie nodded. "And you can tell that old bitch I said so."

"Look, Gracie, be reasonable. You want your job. Jolene wants Roger. The money I'm offering comes from what she paid me to find him. She doesn't have to know you have it. Take the five thousand and Roger and go back to Jolene."

Apparently exhausted from her brisk walk and Roger's frantic wiggling, Gracie plopped on the curb and set him down. He lunged at the squirrel until he almost strangled at the end of his leash, and it skittered up the tree and sat on a low branch, scolding us with its loud chattering. Roger strained at the lead, his feet running, his body going nowhere.

Gracie, looking as deflated as a punctured pool toy, shook her head again, and her lower lip trembled, as if she was ready to cry. "You don't get it. It's a matter of principle. That woman makes my life miserable."

Bribery had failed, so I tried reason. "But you need the job, and she needs you and Roger."

"Jolene and I have had standoffs before, and I've always been the first to blink. Then I go back to her, and although I earn a little more money, she makes my life a bigger hell."

"Then leave Jolene. Give me Roger and use the five thousand to live on until you find another job."

"Who's going to hire me?" I could read genuine fear in her expression. "I'm over-the-hill, overweight and unskilled. Roger is the only leverage I have to make Jolene take me back under my conditions. Because, as much as I need that job, she'll have to promise to treat me right."

"Tell you what." I felt sorry for her, even though her unhappy situation was one she'd helped create. "You make a list of the changes you want in your employment. I'll present your demands to Jolene and see what I can negotiate."

At that point I realized Roger had abandoned the squirrel and was humping my right leg with unbridled enthusiasm.

"Roger!" Gracie screeched and jumped to her feet. "Bad boy!"

I stared down into that upturned, caved-in mug that looked as if he'd hit a wall face-first at sixty miles an hour, and I'd swear his grin had widened. Gracie jerked him away and picked him up again.

"I'll make a list," Gracie promised. "But we're both wasting our time."

She pivoted on her heel and stomped toward the house. Roger grinned at me over her shoulder.

If Gracie was so certain Jolene wasn't going to change, why didn't she either go back to her old employer or get another job?

The obvious answer hit me as I slid behind the wheel of my car.

Apparently Gracie was on spring break.

After leaving Gracie, I took Roosevelt Boulevard toward Tampa. Eastbound traffic on the Howard Franklin Bridge came to a standstill due to an accident at I-275 at the Dale Mabry exit, and I sat for an hour, listening to talk radio and developing a deeper understanding of road rage. If you weren't angry when you climbed into your car, you'd be mad as hell from listening to those guys rant for the length of your commute.

I had switched to Easy Listening when the traffic finally started moving, and fifteen minutes later, I parked in front of Katy's house in Old Hyde Park. Elaine's friend was either making serious money or had inherited a small fortune to afford this pricey piece of real estate, a completely restored bungalow from the arts-and-craft period in one of Tampa's hottest neighborhoods.

Elaine answered the door, dressed in bell-bottom jeans and a tunic top that screamed 1970s. I shivered at the realization that if I lived long enough, I'd probably see all the fashion fads of my youth recycled.

Today Elaine had combed her hair and applied makeup, but her light blue eyes reflected her sorrow.

"Can we talk?" I said.

She motioned toward two cane-bottomed rockers on the wide porch. I sat in one, and she perched on the edge of the seat of the other, pushed her hair off her face and hooked it behind her ears. I caught a glimpse of her palms, pink and smooth with no ligature marks.

"Have you found out who killed my sister?"

"Not yet."

"Then why are you here? I've told you everything I know." Her tone was curious, not accusing.

"Because there's been another murder."

"Like Deirdre's?"

I shook my head. "Where were you yesterday morning around ten o'clock?"

She breathed a shuddering sigh. "At the funeral home, making arrangements for Deirdre's funeral."

"Which funeral home?"

She gave me the name and address. "Why are you questioning me?"

"Because one of the men in Deirdre's newspaper picture was murdered yesterday."

Comprehension flashed in her eyes, as Elaine took less than a second to make the connection. "And you suspect me?"

"Everybody's a suspect for now."

"But I have no link to those men. I don't even know which one Deirdre was looking for." She curled her long, slender fingers into fists. "But if I did, I would have wanted to kill him."

"You haven't thought of anyone else who might have reason to harm Deirdre, someone who might have followed her from Pennsylvania? An old boyfriend? A disgruntled coworker?"

Elaine shook her head. "Deirdre was...withdrawn. I guess her shyness went back to the trauma in her childhood. She kept to herself. Didn't date. Didn't make close friends. She worked in an office where she input computer data, so she didn't interact much with the other employees. When she wasn't working, she stuck close to home and Mom and Dad. After their car crash, Deirdre was alone. That's why she wanted to move back to Tampa, to be with me." Her eyes welled with tears. "Now I'm the one who's alone."

I silently cursed the narcissism and psychopathy of cold-blooded killers that allowed them to inflict such pain on others without suffering the tortures of remorse. They had to have hearts of stone to withstand the backwash of grief and pain from the crimes they committed.

"Ms. Skerritt?" Elaine's voice jerked me from my thoughts. "You're bleeding."

I looked down, then reached into my pocket for a tissue and dabbed at the streaks of blood on the back of my right hand where I'd scratched my hives raw.

"You haven't noticed anyone suspicious around?" I asked. "Anyone following you? Unusual phone calls? Strangers at the door?"

She shook her head. "You're scaring me."

"No need to be frightened. Just stay alert. Deirdre's death may be unrelated to her previous assault. But caution can't hurt."

CHAPTER 9

I believed Elaine's story, but, even so, I checked her alibi with the funeral-home director after I left Hyde Park. He confirmed that Elaine had been where she'd said she was at the time Branigan was murdered, so I headed downtown to Franklin Street and One Police Center.

Abe Mackley, looking harried, haggard and enough like Andy Sipowicz from *NYPD Blue* that he often drew double takes when he appeared on a crime scene, rose from his desk in Investigations to greet me.

Abe had made detective a few years before me and had worked with Bill and me on the child murders sixteen years ago. Last December, Abe had helped us identify and capture Vincent Lovelace's killer and solve several statewide homicides and a case of major insurance fraud. I hadn't seen him since.

"You're a sight for sore eyes, Maggie. You coming back to the Tampa PD now that Pelican Bay's kaput?"

"My police days are over." I gave him one of my cards. "Malcolm and I have opened our own P.I. firm."

"Pelican Bay Investigations," he read with approval and a hint of envy. "I'll be retiring in a few weeks. Let me know if you need another investigator."

"You'll be at the top of our list. You busy?"

He ran a hand over his thinning hair. "Does a bear crap in the woods? There's so much testosterone in the air that I'd bet Viagra sales have dropped statewide. We're working 24/7 to stay on top of these college kids. They started a small riot at Adventure Island yesterday afternoon, resulting in ten arrests. And they trashed a bar in Ybor City last night—fourteen charges—and caused a three Jet Ski DUI collision on the bay this morning, and that's just the tip of the iceberg."

"Ah, spring," I said with a sympathetic smile.

"What I can't figure is where these kids get the

money for all this partying. I never had two dimes to rub together when I was a teen. Hell, I still don't." He shook his head. "But enough bellyaching. What can I do for you?"

I quickly related the details of Deirdre Fisk's murder.

Mackley sighed. "Just when I was sure my give-a-damn's busted, you hit me with this, and it all comes back again. I remember her, a sweet little kid scared out of her mind. I'd give my right arm to catch that son of a bitch. You think the same guy's responsible for her murder?"

I shrugged. "That's why I'm here. I'm hoping something in the old files will point me in the right direction."

"Wait here. I'll get 'em myself. Want some coffee?"

I glanced toward a corner table and the coffee-maker with a month's worth of accumulated crud and grime. "No, thanks. I haven't had my tetanus booster."

Abe grinned. "Same old Maggie. I see you've kept your sense of humor."

"Laughing keeps me out of the shrink's office."

Abe went to retrieve the cold case files, and I stood at the window and surveyed downtown, exploding with growth like the rest of Florida. Several large construction cranes loomed on the skyline where new buildings were going up. I sighed, longing for Florida, B.C. Before condos.

When Abe returned, I told him about Branigan while I copied the files and hoped the Xerox machine, whose workings sounded like the rhythm section of a mariachi band, didn't die on me before I finished.

With the copied files in hand, I drove back across the bay. Investigating Deirdre's murder was on my own time, but I also had a job to do for Stella Branigan. I went directly to Harbor Oaks and Sidney's home next to his parents.

The younger Branigan's abode was a two-story Nantucket-style house with weathered gray cedar shingles and enclosed porches on either side. It looked much more inviting than its pretentious neighbor. If I ignored the palm trees, the place could have been on Martha's Vineyard.

Before knocking on the door, I took a look around. To the left, a tall Surinam cherry hedge blocked the neighboring house and lot from view. To the right, a wide brick walkway through a head-high ligustrum hedge connected Sidney's property with the senior Branigans' house next door. Although the lots were spacious, on a run, someone could cross from one house to the next in less than a minute.

A pleasant-looking woman with rosy cheeks, graying brown hair pulled back in a no-nonsense bun and a welcoming smile answered my knock at the door. She was dressed in a sky-blue utilitarian cotton dress with a crisp white collar. She wore white shoes, the sensible lace-up kind with soft soles.

"I'm Maggie Skerritt." I gave her my card. "I'm investigating Carlton Branigan's murder."

The woman's smile faded, and she opened the door for me to step into the front hall. "I'm Ingrid, the housekeeper. Mr. Sidney is next door with his mother, but Miss Angela's upstairs. I'll let her know you're here."

"Wait, please. If you don't mind, I have a few questions for you first."

Ingrid frowned. "It's not my place—"

"I'm sure Sidney would want you to cooperate in my investigation. And this won't take long."

Ingrid cast a furtive glance up the stairs, then

motioned me into the living room through an arch on the right. Sunlight flooded the cheerful room with its bright cream-white walls and overstuffed sofas and chairs, covered in floral English chintz, clustered around a fireplace with a brick surround and white mantel topped with framed family photos. Above the mantel hung an oil portrait of a chubby toddler in a pink sunbonnet and ruffled sunsuit, wielding her pail and shovel on the beach. The room had a homey, lived-in feel, not the staged, decorator look of many expensive residences.

"You were here yesterday morning?" I asked.

Ingrid nodded. "I come to work at seven, in time to fix breakfast for the family."

"But Mrs. Branigan and her daughter—"

"Brianna."

"Weren't they in Sarasota yesterday?"

"Yes, but Wednesday is my cleaning day, so I came in at my usual time to get a head start."

"And Mr. Branigan was here all morning, too?"

"In his study." Ingrid jerked her thumb toward the sunporch off the living room.

"This is a lovely house." On the pretext of admiring my surroundings, I stepped closer to the study. From its rear windows, most of the backyard of the house next door was visible, although jasmine vines concealed the interior of the arbor where Carlton had died. A door at the back of the room opened to a curving walkway that led around an impressive bed of hybrid tea roses to the garage.

"It was such a terrible tragedy," Ingrid said. "I had just finished cleaning upstairs and turned off the vacuum when the phone rang. It was Mrs. Branigan, screaming for her son to come."

"What happened next?"

"I ran downstairs to the study and told Mr. Sidney his mother needed him. I didn't learn until later, after the police and ambulance arrived, that Mr. Carlton had been murdered."

"It must be hard," I said, "for a young couple to live right next door to one set of in-laws."

Ingrid smiled and shook her head. "You'd think so, but the Branigans get along well." Her smile faded. "Except for Brianna."

"The granddaughter?"

"She's going through a stage, I guess. She just turned nine."

Ingrid picked up a picture in a silver frame from

Sidney's large desk and handed it to me. Fortunately Brianna hadn't inherited her grandmother's and Sidney's horsey features. A pretty child with long blond hair and deep blue eyes gazed back at me.

"What kind of stage?" I asked.

"She sulks in her room a lot and doesn't like to visit her grandparents like she used to. I suppose at her age she's more interested in talking to her friends on the telephone than being around old folks."

I returned the frame to Sidney's desk. "Did you notice anything suspicious next door yesterday morning? See anyone coming or going?"

"I was so busy cleaning, what with the vacuum cleaner noise and all, a tornado could have struck next door, and I wouldn't have known it." Ingrid's kind eyes misted with tears. "I wish I could help. The Branigans have been good to me, and I hate that this has happened. I hope you find the killer."

"Would you ask Mrs. Branigan if she'll see me now?"

"Of course."

Ingrid left the room, and I heard her soft steps on the stairs. Moments later, Angela Branigan entered the room. A tiny slip of a woman with straight blond hair and blue eyes that she'd passed on to her daughter, she wore a simple black dress, black stockings and shoes, and a silver chain with a sterling Celtic cross. Her face was pale, and despite her attempts at composure, her nervousness was obvious.

But I'd be nervous, too, if my father-in-law had been brutally murdered within shouting distance of my home.

"I apologize for intruding at a time like this," I said, "but your mother-in-law has hired me to investigate her husband's death."

Angela sank into one of the deep chintz-covered chairs, looking like an inkblot against the vibrant floral, and clasped her trembling hands in her lap. "I don't know how I can help. I wasn't even here."

"But you and your in-laws are close?"

Her face spasmed in an expression that could have been grief or distaste before she regained her neutral facade. "We practically live in each other's pockets, as you can see."

She'd mentioned physical proximity, but had avoided describing their emotional ties.

"Do you know of anyone," I said, "who'd want to harm the senator?"

She laughed, a harsh sound, like a barking dog. "Only half the state. He was a politician, after all."

Half the state was too many suspects to eliminate. I hoped Bill was having better luck with Carlton's aides. "But no one specific?"

She paused before answering, as if choosing her words carefully. "Carlton had one of those personalities that you either loved or despised."

"Which was it with you?"

Her only reply was a slight flaring of her delicate nostrils.

"If you'll excuse me—" She rose from her chair with a graceful, fluid motion and one hand clutching her cross. "I must check on my daughter. Her grandfather's murder has upset Brianna so terribly, her pediatrician had to sedate her. She's sleeping now, but I want to be there when she awakens."

Worry furrowed the smooth skin of her brow and deepened the blue in her eyes. She seemed genuinely concerned for her daughter.

"Thank you for your time," I said, "and I'm sorry for your loss."

"Ingrid will see you out." Taking slow, careful strides as if trying to keep from hurrying, Angela walked from the room and up the stairs.

After Ingrid closed the front door behind me, I considered the strange vibes I'd picked up from Angela Branigan. Although she'd dressed the part of grieving relative, she hadn't seemed all that sorry that her father-in-law was dead and had sidestepped my question on her opinion of Carlton. But disliking her in-laws didn't make her a murderer, and she'd been sixty miles away at the time of her father-in-law's death.

Something was amiss in that household. I could feel it in the air. But my goal was to find a killer, not investigate the lack of domestic tranquillity in Sidney Branigan's home.

CHAPTER 10

Rather than return to my car, I strolled past the front of Sidney's house, took a walkway to the backyard, ambled through the hedge that marked the property line, and approached the arbor where Carlton had died. The CSU techs had completed their investigation and removed their crime-scene tape, but I wanted to experience the lay of the land again and form my own conclusions.

From inside the arbor, I could see the tennis court at one end and the pool at the other, but the thick jasmine vines obscured the back of the house. A seawall edged the property along the waterfront, and a large dock with davits extended into the harbor. The killer could have come and gone by boat, but Stella would have noticed its approach and the noise of engines from her upstairs window. I'd check the wind speeds from yesterday morning, but if they'd been calm like today's, a sailboat would have taken forever to make a getaway and would have been spotted, tacking toward the channel, even after the police arrived.

The sound of heated voices on the terrace above me cut through the quiet, and I recognized Sidney's voice.

"Why waste money on a private detective?" He sounded angry.

"Because the police are treating your father's murder as just any other case," Stella answered in her haughty manner. "He deserves better."

"Some people may think he already got what he deserved." His words held weariness and pain.

I could hear Stella sputtering, groping for words. "How dare you say that?"

"Get off your high horse, Mother. It's me you're talking to, not a campaign crowd. You know Dad climbed to the top on a lot of people's backs. He was self-centered and ruthless."

"Have you no respect for your father's memory?" Stella said in a shrill tone.

"You're planning to make a public spectacle of his funeral," Sidney replied, as if speaking were an effort. "He was just a man, for God's sake, a flawed man, not a saint."

"He was a great man, and he would have been greater—" Stella's voice broke with a sob "—if someone hadn't cut him down on his rise to the top."

"Why don't we have a private family service?" Sidney had lowered his voice and added persuasion. "It will be easier on all of us, especially Brianna. Her doctor has sedated her, she's so upset."

"Death is a fact of life Brianna must learn to face," Stella said. "And your father had so many people who loved him, not allowing them to pay their final respects would be cruel."

"Cruel? Isn't what you're doing to your grand-daughter cruel?"

"You coddle that child, Sidney. As much as Carlton adored her, you let her stay away from him too often in his last days. How could you?"

Sidney made a noise of obvious disgust, and foot-steps stomped off the terrace and up the path toward the house next door.

I heard the house door off the terrace open and close, and, after waiting a moment for the coast to clear, I made my way out of the arbor back to where my car was parked in Sidney's driveway. I was opening my door when a voice interrupted.

"What the hell are you doing in my yard?" Sidney, eyes blazing, strode toward me.

I shut the door and turned to meet him. "Your mother hired me to investigate your father's murder."

"Not at my house you don't. My wife and daughter are upset enough without your bothering them."

"I'm just leaving."

"Don't come back, or I'll get a restraining order."

Sidney's reaction, both earlier on the terrace and now, wasn't what I'd expected. His face was flushed, his respiration ragged and his fists clenched. A hint of fear flashed along with the anger in his eyes. And beneath the fear and rage lurked that haunted look I'd seen too often in survivors when death has taken someone close by surprise.

"What are you afraid I'll find?" I asked, making a stab in the dark.

He struggled visibly for self-control, and when he

finally spoke, his voice was calmer. "There's nothing *to* find. If you really want to know what happened to my father, you're wasting your time—and my mother's money—here."

"You didn't see anyone or anything out of the ordinary yesterday morning?"

"My father lying dead in his own backyard was extraordinary enough."

"Before that?"

"I was working. I had my back to the break in the hedge. I wasn't even aware George Ulrich had come and gone until Mother told me."

Sidney protested too much. He apparently held secrets he didn't want uncovered, but I'd need more digging to determine whether what he was concealing involved his father's murder or merely the kind of private idiosyncrasies that all families guarded. I climbed into my car and drove away. In the rearview mirror, I saw Sidney, hands on his hips, watching, until I pulled onto the street.

I considered stopping by the hospital to check on Mother, but I might not be lucky enough to find her sleeping this time. My emotions were raw from

Seton Fellows's revelations, and I didn't know how I'd react to her with my present knowledge. I rationalized that I didn't want to cause her distress that might impede her recovery. I wanted to share what I'd learned from Seton with Bill—we'd been too involved with our current case for me to bring it up before now—and hear his advice in hopes it would keep me from making my relationship with Mother worse than it already was.

But concern for her was only half the issue. The rest of the story was that I was flat-out chicken. Almost fifty, I still felt like a child, caught with my hand in the cookie jar, whenever I was with my mother.

Darcy had already gone home when I reached the office, but Bill was waiting with a huge wicker picnic basket in the middle of his desk. Its presence reminded me that I'd forgotten to eat lunch.

"How come every time we're together, there's food involved?" I asked.

He lifted his eyebrows and threw me the grin that never failed to make my knees weak. "Because I know your weakness?"

"Every man on the street knows my weakness. All he has to do is look at the size of my hips."

"You have delectable hips, Margaret, and I'll punch the next guy I catch looking at them."

"My hero," I said with an exaggerated sigh, and batted my eyelashes.

"You talking about me or a sandwich?"

"See, it's always about food."

"But food is so sensual." His grin widened.

"Not the kind in my refrigerator."

"That's not food. That's desperation."

"Speaking of desperation, what's in the basket? I'm starving."

"I thought you were worried about your hips."

"For now, they're on their own. Are we eating here?"

He shook his head. "The weather's perfect to enjoy one of the perks of this office."

"The rooftop deck?"

"Lead the way. I'll follow with the food."

I went into the hall to an outer door that opened to an exterior staircase. The owners of the bookstore below had originally constructed the rooftop deck in hopes customers would take their books and coffee up to enjoy the view. Newcomers to Florida, they hadn't realized that most days the deck would be too hot, too cold, too windy or too bug-infested to enjoy. Once they'd caught on, they'd closed off the ground-level stairs. Now the deck was accessible only from the second floor. And today was one of a handful out of the year that the climate favored use of the rooftop patio with its unique view of the bay and the setting sun.

The bookstore folks had left the wrought-iron tables and chairs and planters filled with palms and exotic shrubs, and the roof provided a perfect oasis for a sunset picnic, if you ignored the occasional gasoline fumes that wafted on the updraft.

"The reason our being together usually involves food," Bill said, as he spread a supper of his famous chicken salad with white grapes and almonds, a soft, Italian herb bread, and a chilled Riesling, "is that the only times we get together is over meals. As soon as the business gets on its feet, we'll pick and choose our cases more carefully, so we'll have more free time."

With two murders under investigation, free time was an alien concept. I took a sip of wine. "I spoke with Elaine this morning—"

He raised his hand and cut me off, firmly but gently. "Enjoy your meal. We'll talk about the case later."

But later, we talked about Mother. I related to Bill what Dr. Fellows had told me about her insecurities and her jealousy of me. Sharing my distress with someone I trusted, someone who understood me, felt good.

"So," I said after I'd finished my story, "what do I do now?"

He swirled his wine in his glass and thought for a moment. "Nothing's changed with your mother, except her state of health. She apparently feels the same as she always has about you. But that's her problem, not yours."

"Of course it's my problem!"

He smiled and squeezed my hand across the table. "You're not the *cause* of the problem. The cause lies within Priscilla. But you *can* choose how you react to her insecurities."

"What do you mean?"

"Don't take her attitude personally."

"But she's my mother!" If he'd been any other man, I would have dismissed his advice as callous, but Bill understood human behavior and motivations better than most psychiatrists, so I didn't blow off his words. With a friend like Bill, I didn't need a therapist, not if I paid attention.

"Her lack of affection and approval is tragic," he said, "but it's also a fact you've lived with all your life. In that sense, nothing's new. Except that now you're relieved of the burden of believing that such a lack is your fault. Treat her with respect, and even pity, but don't let her drag you down."

I took another drink of wine. "That's easier said than done."

"I know. Because she's your mother, and mothers are supposed to love their children. But you've worked enough abuse cases to know better. Did the children we rescued deserve what their mothers did to them?"

"Of course not."

"I rest my case."

Intellectually, I knew Bill was right, but comprehending that fact emotionally was tougher. My inner child still longed for a mommy who loved me without reservation. The adult me was thankful for Bill, whose love was unconditional. Even on my worst days, he'd been there for me. Maybe in the cosmic scheme of things, he was in my life to make up for what I'd missed. Whatever the reason, I was lucky to have him.

"Mother insisted before Christmas that she

didn't want to see me again. That gives me an out to avoid her."

Bill nodded. "But would avoiding her make you happy?"

"On one level." I could never lie to Bill, not only because I loved him, but also because he'd know I wasn't being honest. "Ignoring a problem is always a seductive choice. But she is my mother, and Caroline and I are all she has."

"You'll make the right decision. Just don't let her manipulate you with guilt. You have nothing to feel guilty about."

I sank back in my chair and watched the last remnants of spectacular colors play across the western horizon. Bill pulled his chair beside mine and slid his arm around my shoulders. The wine was working the kinks out of my muscles, and my eyelids were drooping when Bill's cell phone rang, spoiling the mood.

"That," I said with a scowl, "is why I don't want one of those damned things. Don't answer it."

He pulled the phone from his pocket and checked the caller ID. "It's Adler."

Curiosity trumped my irritation. "Go ahead, see what he wants."

Bill took the call, spoke a few words and slipped the phone back into his pocket. "He has the autopsy results on Carlton Branigan and says he'll fill us in, if we want to come over for coffee."

"That'll work. We can all share what we learned today."

"And Sharon baked a cake."

I scowled and quoted one of Estelle's favorite Bible verses. "'Get thee behind me, Satan.' And he always does—and plants a few pounds on my butt while he's back there."

Bill pulled me to him and kissed me. "You've been paranoid about your weight ever since the diet clinic murders. But you mustn't worry. You're perfect, just the way you are."

I leaned back in his arms and grinned. "Then let us eat cake."

CHAPTER 11

Adler lived in a southside Pelican Bay neighborhood in a gray clapboard house with black shutters and a wide front porch that stretched across the front like open arms. The porch light illuminated rocking chairs, an old-fashioned swing, pots of red geraniums and a toddler-size tricycle. Although the place was small—most cops couldn't afford bigger—Adler and Sharon had done the renovating themselves and created an updated, cozy home.

Bill parked his new SUV, what I called his Macho Machine, at the front curb and looked around through the gathering twilight.

"This is a great neighborhood," he said. "How'd you like to live here?"

Having visited the Adlers often, I was familiar

with the area. "Lots of families with young children. It might be too noisy for a couple of old fogies like us."

Bill laughed. "You're barely forty-nine. In Florida, you're not an old fogy until at least eighty-five."

"But, you have to admit, we are accustomed to our peace and quiet."

But only in our off-hours. Between us, we'd witnessed too much death, destruction and pain, with Deirdre Fisk and Carlton Branigan and the ripple effect of their murders on their families only the latest examples. Maybe that's why I felt so old.

And maybe that's why living in a neighborhood filled with young couples and children would be good for me. I'd promised myself when I'd agreed to marry Bill that I'd learn to lighten up. I decided to rethink my reservations about living in a subdivision. Surrounding myself with young lives and laughter might be a good start to adjusting my attitude.

"It wouldn't hurt to check with a real-estate agent and find out what's available," I said.

He glanced at me in surprise. "You're serious?"

"We have to live somewhere. This neighborhood is close to the office and the marina."

I waited for the wave of panic that usually followed any thought of permanently blending my life with Bill's, but tonight it didn't come.

I did, however, jump in alarm when someone rapped on my window. Adler was standing beside the SUV, so I opened the door.

"You two coming in?" he asked, "or were you planning to sit here and neck like a couple of teenagers?"

"Not with an audience." Bill climbed out, shut the door and, after I climbed out, keyed the lock. "That spoils the fun."

We followed Adler up the walk, and Sharon, petite with green eyes and dark brown hair, met us at the door with a welcoming smile.

"Coffee's almost ready," she said. "Come into the kitchen."

The Adlers had taken out a wall between two rooms at the back of the house, so their kitchen and family room flowed into one large space that opened onto the backyard through a wall of French doors. A pine table centered the eat-in kitchen that smelled of oranges, the same aroma that used to fill the air from the juice concentrate processing plant in Dunedin before the citrus groves' demise.

Bill and I settled at the table across from Adler, and Sharon served mugs of coffee and thick slices of glazed orange-chiffon cake before slipping away to check on Jessica, asleep in the nursery.

Between bites of cake that melted in my mouth, I told Adler and Bill about my visit with Elaine Fisk and checking out her alibi.

"I doubt our killer could have been Elaine, or George Ulrich," Adler said. "Not after the autopsy results."

"Why not?" Bill asked.

"Doc found the victim's hyoid cartilage and larynx completely shattered. From the angle of the ligature marks on his throat, she thinks someone close to Branigan's height must have strangled him."

"What if he was knocked to his knees?" I asked.

Adler shook his head. "I asked the same question. Doc pointed out that, if he'd fallen to the ground during a struggle, Branigan's bare knees would have been more abraded. From the state of his skin and the lack of bleeding on his legs, she thinks he was dead before he hit the ground."

"Stella Branigan's a tall woman," I said.

"But she was in her room until minutes before finding the body," Adler said. "Porter grilled the butler hard. Madison insists he took the wife coffee right after Ulrich left. And a cleaning lady, working upstairs, corroborates that Mrs. Branigan was in her room the entire time she said she was. So she couldn't have been our killer."

"Besides," Bill added, "if Stella's the killer, why would she hire us? She's aware that we know what we're doing and would collar her eventually."

"You're right," I said. "But what about Sidney? He's tall enough, and he acts as if he's hiding something."

"We checked his hands," Adler said. "They're clean. If he's our perp, he would have had to have worn gloves to the arbor, intending to kill his father with the vine, then returned home and ditched the gloves—and changed his bloody clothes—before responding to his mother's call. But I haven't been able to come up with a motive for Sidney. Therefore, no compelling reason for a search warrant."

"Something's not right in that family," I said. "Sidney's housekeeper told me his nine-year-old daughter has refused to visit her grandparents recently. What kid that age doesn't like her grandparents?"

"Stella Branigan isn't your typical warm and cuddly grandma," Adler said.

Bill caught my eye across the table. "Or maybe Grandpa was too warm and cuddly."

I nodded. "That would fit, especially if he's the sexual predator we're looking for. Brianna's the same age and appearance as the other victims. I brought copies of the cold cases back from Tampa. Bill and I will look through them tonight to see what else we can find."

"Any chance you could question Brianna about her grandfather?" Bill asked Adler.

"Not without one of her parents present," he said.

"I don't think Sidney would agree." No longer a cop, however, I was under no such restriction. "Maybe I can talk with her."

"Without the parents?" Adler said.

"I can try. From what I overheard Sidney saying today, I doubt Brianna will be at the funeral. He said it would be too stressful for her. Maybe the housekeeper will let me talk to the girl while the parents are at the reception after the services. Has Doc released Branigan's body?"

Adler nodded. "Funeral's scheduled for day after tomorrow."

"I'll see what I can do. What about physical evidence? Did the techs find anything?"

Adler nodded. "Fibers in the vine around the vic's neck. They traced them to garden gloves sold by the hundreds at Home Depot. No matching gloves found on the property."

I raised my eyebrows. "That's it?"

"That's it. And the ballistics report is in on the Fisk bullet. No match in the system."

Bill finished his coffee and put down his mug. "Branigan's aide gave me the names of a few possible suspects. Top of the list is a radical feminist in Belleair, who's sent death threats to Branigan because of his conservative voting record. Also, a man in Safety Harbor, who claims he lost his job as the result of some environmental legislation Branigan sponsored, and an Hispanic day laborer, angry over the senator's vote on a bill that adversely affected migrant workers."

Adler took a small notebook from his pocket and

scribbled the names Bill gave him. "Porter and I will check these out."

"I'm still thinking Branigan's and Deirdre's murders are connected," I said, "but damned if I can figure out how."

Sharon returned to the kitchen. "Jessica woke up and wanted to come out and play. I just got her back to sleep. Anyone want more coffee?"

"No thanks." I stood and gave Bill a look. Adler and Sharon had precious little time together, and I didn't want to infringe on it any longer. "We have to go."

Adler showed us to the door. "Keep in touch."

"You have plans?" I asked Bill as he pulled away from the curb.

"Yeah." He flashed a wicked grin. "I'm hoping to get lucky. You wanna play?"

"Yes," I said, "and Crest Lake Park has a playground."

His grin faded. "Where Deirdre Fisk was murdered?"

I nodded. "Let's snoop around. Some of the regulars may have seen something and might be more willing to talk to us than the cops."

"It's worth a try. But not half as much fun as what I had in mind." He threaded his way through Adler's subdivision to Highland Avenue and headed south into Clearwater. At Cleveland Street, he hung a left and drove the short distance to the park, a city block centered with a small lake surrounded by wide grassy spaces intersected by jogging trails. An attractive recreational area in daylight, once the sun went down, the park took on a sinister aspect and filled with unsavory creatures.

Bill parked and we both got out.

"I may have better luck talking to the working girls if I'm alone." I pulled a hundred-dollar bill from my wallet and folded it so that Benjamin's face was visible. "To grease the skids."

"I'll stay within sight of you. Holler if you need me."

I struck out along the path. Toward the center of the park, I spotted a woman sitting on a bench that overlooked the lake. I sauntered past her, then sat on the other end of the bench. Farther back along the walkway where I'd come, Bill knelt as if tying his shoe.

In the faint glow of streetlights, I could observe

the woman's outrageous attire: hot pants so low on her hips and cut so high on her legs that her belt was almost as wide as her shorts, four-inch wedge-heeled shoes, and a sequin-spangled halter top that left her midriff, shoulders and cleavage bare. Even in the dim light, her black-rimmed eyes and thick false eyelashes were plainly visible beneath her huge pouf of teased blond hair.

"I'm working this park," she warned. "This is my spot. Go find your own." Between the thick layer of makeup and the poor lighting, I couldn't see her skin that clearly, but her voice made her sound young, still in her teens.

I thought of my friend Karen Longwood, the psychologist from the weight-loss clinic, who was setting up a mentoring program for at-risk children. For the past few months, Karen had been whacking her way through bureaucratic red tape, while every day, more and more children without proper role models and supervision were falling through the cracks. I'd arrested too many of them in my days as a cop, and for a fleeting instant, I was glad I had no authority to arrest this one, a girl who should have been at home watching TV with her family or chatting on the phone with her friends, not turning tricks on a park bench.

I flashed my folded bill. "I'm paying, not working."

"I don't do women."

"I'm looking for information, not sex."

She appeared ready to run, but she wouldn't get far in those shoes. "You a cop?"

"Private detective. Were you working here Monday night?"

"All the nights seem the same to me." Unlike earlier, she now sounded old and tired.

"Were you here the night the woman was killed, just over there?" I pointed to where Adler had said Deirdre's body was found.

"What if I was?"

"You see anything?"

"Nothing I'd testify to in court."

"Anything that might help me find a killer?"

She shrugged, but I could tell she had her eye on the bill in my hand. I considered the probability that she'd lie for the money but decided to take that chance. I waited, watching the reflection of the cylindrical city water tower on the lake's smooth surface.

Several yards away, Bill had left the path and

wandered to the edge of the lake. He hadn't looked my way, but I knew he was watching, aware of every movement. As long as he had my back, I was in no danger.

"I saw what happened," she finally said.

I had to strain to hear, because her voice had dropped to barely above a whisper.

"Afterward?"

She shook her head. "I was over in the bushes there, taking a pee. The girl that was murdered was waiting on the bench near where the cops found her. She got up and waved when she saw the killer coming."

"She knew her killer?"

"Looked like she'd been waiting for him."

"What did he look like?"

"A tall man, wearing loose slacks and a jacket. And sneakers."

"Did you see his face?"

"He wore a ball cap with the brim pulled down. And he had on sunglasses, even though it was night."

"Could you tell anything else about him? His age? His race?"

"He was a white guy, but I dunno his age. He

moved in long, easy steps, like an athlete, not an old man."

I was beginning to think the working girl was jerking my chain—until she spoke again.

"So anyway, the girl on the bench sees this guy coming and waves and jumps up to meet him. The guy walks right up to her, pulls a gun from his pocket, sticks it under the girl's chin and fires. It's a good thing I'd just peed, or I'd have wet my pants."

The hooker had described the killing almost exactly as Doc Cline and I had reconstructed it. "What happened next?"

"The killer leaned down, as if to make sure the girl was dead, then just walked back the way he'd come."

"Did he get in a car? Take a cab?"

"I dunno. I was so scared, I ran the other way. Didn't come back here for two whole nights."

I remembered Deirdre Fisk's empty wallet. "But you took the girl's money first."

"What if I did?" Her voice was cold, defiant. "She sure didn't need it anymore. I did." She nodded toward the bill in my hand. "That's the only reason I'm talking to you now."

"You've never been arrested, have you?"

She jerked her head up and stared at me. "I thought you weren't a cop. You taking me in?"

I shook my head. "Your prints were on the wallet. They're not in the system." I softened my voice. "You don't have a record yet, so it's not too late. Find yourself another job. Clean up your act. This life will kill you, one way or another, and you're too young to die."

She turned away, but I could see the tears glistening in her eyes. "It's not that easy."

"Not easy, but possible. But if you decide to try, call me, and I'll see what I can do to help." I handed her the money and my card. "Thanks for the information. It's more than we knew before."

The hooker tucked the bill into her halter. "Could you leave now? You're hurting business."

Frustrated by the conviction that I'd never hear from her, I joined Bill at the water's edge and told him what I'd learned.

We spent the next hour canvassing the night life in the area, but no one else had seen the guy the hooker had described in the park Monday night. They'd all been asleep, too stoned, too drunk or too leery of getting involved.

CHAPTER 12

My alarm sounded at seven-thirty the next morning, and I reluctantly dragged myself from bed. After dropping me off at the office to pick up my car, Bill had returned to my condo to study the cold case files with me, but, exhausted, he'd left before I went to bed, not that long ago.

Some trips down memory lane are pleasant. Last night's wasn't. We'd been up until four in the morning, guzzling too much coffee and reading the grisly details of crimes so horrible I wished I hadn't encountered them the first time, much less revisited them. I had filled a few pages of a legal pad with notes and follow-up questions before finally conceding brain death, walking Bill to the door, kissing him good-night and turning in.

Not sure my brain had been resurrected by a mere three hours' sleep, I hit the shower, then slathered on half a bottle of calamine lotion to soothe my raging hives before I dressed. Over coffee, I made a call to Doc Cline to tell her what Bill and I had run across in the files last night that might prove useful.

"You're at work early," I said.

"I have a whopper of a backlog. What's up?"

"Did you run a DNA screen on Branigan?"

"Yeah, to check the hairs we found on his shirt, but according to the DNA, they belong to the vic."

"I have a DNA report from my cold cases. Its source isn't in any of the data banks, so there's no one to connect it to. If I fax you the info, can you compare it with Branigan's DNA?"

"Sure, but you know the drill, Maggie. Unless it's related to a current investigation, it will have to go to the end of the line."

"I have no problem waiting. After sixteen years, what's a few more days? I have an errand to run this morning, so I'll fax the report when I get back to my office."

By eight-thirty I was in my car driving into Clearwater. Once I arrived downtown, I parked on the third level of a parking garage near the intersection of Cleveland and Fort Harrison and entered a mostly deserted office building. Downtown had been in decline for years, no longer the bustling center of commerce I remembered from my youth. All the action, with the exception of the Church of Scientology headquarters and classrooms, was either in outlying malls or on Clearwater Beach.

A dark hallway led from the garage to an office overlooking an alley. Facts, Inc., was owned by Archer Phillips, an old high-school classmate of mine, who ran a computer business, searching records of all kinds, primarily for insurance companies, personnel departments of large corporations and the occasional private detective who could afford Archer's exorbitant fees.

While working on the diet-clinic murders last year, I'd called in a favor from Archer. His work had settled his debt with me, so any request I made this morning would go on my tab, and, since Bill and I were investigating the Fisk murder without a paying client, the fee would come from my pocket. But at this point, I was willing to mortgage my condo if it meant catching the monster who had killed those little girls years ago.

Archer's mother, a tiny, dried-up little woman who ran Archer's office, as well as every other aspect of his life, greeted me at the reception desk.

"Margaret Skerritt! What brings you here? I thought the Pelican Bay Police Department closed."

"They did. I'm here to see Archer."

Her eyes narrowed with suspicion. "A social call?"

Poor Archer had never had a chance. Besides being awkward and unattractive, he'd had his mother running interference with every woman who'd ever shown an interest in him—except the woman in his clandestine love nest in a condo in Pelican Bay, whom his dear mama didn't know existed. I, however, had stumbled across Archer's secret during a stakeout years ago and had guarded his privacy in return for information he'd supplied on some murder suspects.

"No need to worry, Mrs. Phillips, this is strictly professional. I'm in business for myself now."

She studied me with mistrust over the gold-wire frames of her thick glasses. "What kind of business?"

I handed her my card. "Pelican Bay Investigations."

She took the card, but her gaze lighted on the ring on my left hand. "Is that what I think it is?"

Bill had given me the yellow gold band set with three aquamarines, my birthstone, for Christmas as a symbol of our engagement. "I'm getting married next year," I said, "to my business partner."

"Best wishes, dear." She exhaled with obvious relief, and the tension left her bony shoulders. "I'll tell Archer you're here."

She rose from her desk, stepped inside the room behind her for a moment, then returned and motioned me into Archer's office.

Archer stood when I entered and waved me to a chair in front of his desk. "Thanks, Mama. I'll call if I need you."

Mrs. Phillips's skepticism had returned, and with a warning glance at me over her shoulder, she closed the door. Why she believed every woman on earth was out to seduce her son, I had no idea. With his thick lips, small eyes, pear-shaped body, tiny feet, and a wardrobe that consisted solely of polyester slacks, pastel guayaberas and sandals, he was almost a caricature of a man, and without the benefit of an endearing personality to offset his liabilities.

He'd begun to sweat as soon as I entered the room,

and he waved my card his mother had given him. "Still a dick, eh, Margaret?"

"No need to worry, Archer, your secret's safe with me."

His thick lips turned downward. "I don't have a secret anymore. She left me."

"I'm sorry to hear that." And I was. Archer's mother had obviously made his life hell, and he'd deserved his little bit of happiness on the side. "I'm not here to blackmail you. This time I brought my checkbook."

At the mention of money, his expression brightened. "What have you got, another murder suspect?"

I nodded. "Carlton Branigan."

"The senator?" His beady eyes widened in surprise. "He's dead."

"And he took all his secrets with him. I'm hoping you can unearth a few for me."

Archer frowned. "Will this be confidential? The Branigans have a lot of clout in this town. I don't want my business ruined."

"Most of what I'm looking for is available in public documents. I just need you to find it. Whatever turns up will never be attributed to you."

I filled him in on the Tampa cold cases and Deirdre Fisk's recent murder.

"And you think Branigan was involved?" Archer looked disbelieving.

"I know he didn't kill Deirdre. He was in Tallahassee at the time of her death. But if he's connected to the murders of those young girls, I may have a better handle on who shot Deirdre. And who might have killed Branigan and why."

He hesitated, as if considering his options, then, with his eye on my checkbook, asked, "What kind of info are you looking for?"

I handed him a list of dates and questions Bill and I had compiled last night while studying the old files. "These are the dates the girls were murdered. I need you to cross-reference them to Branigan. He was a public figure even back then, so his comings and goings and the meetings he attended were chronicled in the news and public records. I want to know where he was when those girls died. And also what kind of car he was driving."

"Some of that info won't be online."

"If not, it should be on microfiche at the courthouse and library or the newspaper offices."

"You're an ex-librarian. Why can't you handle this?"

Because I was supposed to be solving Branigan's murder for his wife and retrieving a kidnapped dog for Jolene Jernigan. And yesterday Bill had picked up several workmen's comp claims for us to investigate for an insurance company. "You don't want the job?"

"Sure, but it'll cost you."

"I'll give you a check for five hundred. Once you've used that up, you can bill me another five hundred, but let me know what you've found before continuing past that amount." I wrote the check and handed it to him. "Can you make this a priority?"

He shrugged his sloping shoulders. "If what you're looking for isn't online, finding it could take time."

"I'm looking for a killer, one who could strike again, so the sooner you get started, the better."

He slid the check into the top drawer of his desk. "I'll put you at the top of the list."

"Don't get up," I said. "I'll show myself out."

Mrs. Phillips eyed me as I passed her desk. "Margaret, this is for you."

She passed me a pink business card as if it were the key to the DaVinci Code.

"What's this?" I asked.

She pointed to my calamine-streaked face. "It's the name and number of my Mary Kay rep. You really have to do something about your makeup, dear. I don't see how you caught a man, but you won't keep him, looking like that."

I wanted to talk with Stella Branigan about her husband's murder, so I turned south out of the parking garage and drove the few short miles to Harbor Oaks. A caterer's van was parked in the circular driveway in front of the Branigan house, and I pulled in behind it.

Madison, looking as if every piece of clothing, from his well-cut navy suit and tie to his white shirt with French cuffs, had too much starch, answered my ring at the front door and looked down his nose at me. "Mrs. Branigan is busy."

"I'll wait. In fact, I'd like to talk with you."

He shook his head. "I've told the police everything I know."

"But I'm not with the police. Mrs. Branigan hired me to investigate her husband's murder. Shall I tell her you refuse to cooperate?"

Looking cornered and unhappy, he conceded. "What do you want to know?"

"Where were you Monday night?"

"Monday is my night off."

"Do you live on the premises?"

"Yes, but what has Monday got to do with anything? Mr. Branigan died Wednesday morning."

"Humor me. Where were you Monday night?"

"I wasn't here. I had a…meeting with a friend."

Madison's entire body language screamed deception, and I recalled the hooker's description of Deirdre's killer, one that could fit Madison in the proper clothes. Would he have killed Deirdre to protect his employer?

"Can this friend verify where you were and when?"

The butler's face turned beet-red. "You are not an officer. You have no authority to question me."

"Fine. I'll have Mrs. Branigan ask you."

"No, wait." He took a deep breath and gave me the name of a gay watering hole in Dunedin. "The bartender there can vouch for me. I'd rather not have my friend involved."

I wrote the name of the bar in the notebook I carried in my blazer, not chancing the information to the mercy of my short-term memory. As I shoved the notes back into my pocket, Stella entered from the back of the house. A young woman, dressed in a dark pants suit and low-heeled shoes and moving with brisk efficiency, accompanied her.

"Remember," Stella was saying, "I want the table decor and the food presentation subdued, but nothing drab or dreary. All in the best of taste. We're celebrating my husband's life, after all."

"Of course, Mrs. Branigan," the woman said. "I'll prepare some sample menus as soon as I return to the office and fax them to you."

"And will you have time to prepare," Stella said, "so that all will be ready when we return after the funeral tomorrow?"

"I'll hire extra help if needed," the caterer said. "You won't be disappointed."

Madison pivoted on his heel as if relieved to escape me and hurried to open the door for the departing caterer. Stella seemed to notice me for the first time.

With her black silk dress accentuating her pallor, she appeared every inch the grieving widow. Shadows beneath her eyes denoted lack of sleep, and she clasped a linen handkerchief in one hand, ready for tears, whose previous appearance had already streaked the coral blush on her cheeks. Although her dress and shoes were impeccable and every hair was in place, she looked harried and slightly befuddled.

"Hello, Margaret. I'm sorry to keep you waiting, but I'm expecting several hundred people after the funeral tomorrow, and there's so little time to plan."

"I know you're busy, but if you could answer a few questions, you could help with my investigation."

"Of course."

She gestured toward the living room, and I preceded her into the space where Carlton's portrait gazed down on us from above the mantel. I sat on the sofa, and Stella sank into a chair as if her legs had given way. She reached into a sterling silver box, retrieved a cigarette and lit it with a matching silver lighter.

After filling her lungs with smoke, she slowly exhaled. "Have you any idea yet who killed my husband?"

"We're checking into several suspects who threatened him in the past."

"George Ulrich?" Her lips twitched if his name left a bad taste in her mouth.

"The police have questioned him, but his involvement seems unlikely."

Stella shook her head, her eyes dazed. "I still can't believe it. Carlton was so alive, so vibrant, with so much he wanted to do in life. I still expect to see him striding through the door, ready for the next challenge."

"How did he and Sidney get along?"

Her eyes cleared and she smiled. "They were very close. Sidney worshipped his father, and Carlton was proud of his son."

"No tensions or arguments?"

She shook her head, seemingly undisturbed by my line of questioning. "The only problem Sidney ever had with Carlton was that his father was away so much, especially while Sidney was growing up. As a little boy, all Sidney ever wanted was to spend time with Carlton and be just like him."

"And now?"

"They spent whatever time they could together, but with Carlton in Tallahassee so much of the year and Sidney with his own family to occupy him…"

Her voice trailed off, her lips quivered, and tears welled in her eyes. She dabbed at them with her linen handkerchief. "Poor Sidney. Carlton's death has devastated him."

If a family feud had existed, I couldn't prove it by Stella. I was running into dead ends every direction I turned. "Can you think of any enemies, other than the political ones I mentioned, who would have wanted Carlton dead?"

She shook her head and smiled through her tears. "Carlton had a warm, wonderful personality that drew people like a magnet. Even his opponents liked him."

With a few notable exceptions, I thought, the main one being whoever had strangled him to death in a rage. And if that person was merely an anonymous face in the crowd, someone who had stepped briefly into the life of a man known to his assailant only through the media, finding that killer would be like searching for a specific grain of sand on a broad beach.

"Thanks for your help."

I rose to my feet and headed toward the door. If I intended to find Carlton Branigan's killer, I had a lot of sifting to do.

CHAPTER 13

After turning up nada during my interview with Stella, I pointed my trusty Volvo toward Pelican Bay and the hospital. Although I'd visited since Mother had been admitted, I hadn't actually spoken with her yet, and, except for Caroline's assurances, Mother didn't know I'd been there. I found myself confronted with a lose/lose scenario. She didn't really want to see me, but she'd be even more pissed off if I didn't show up to pay my respects.

I was waiting for the light at Fort Harrison and Turner and contemplating that sad state of affairs, when brakes squealed behind me, and I was jolted by the impact of a vehicle that had rear-ended mine. In an instant, the force of the collision threw my body against the seat belt, and my head whiplashed against the headrest.

Already irritated by three investigations that were going nowhere fast and the prospect of a visit with my mother, I threw the gearshift into Park, switched off the engine, stepped out of the car and walked toward the back of it. A sporty, small-sized SUV had struck my rear bumper, and my usual patience, which I'd sustained with care during my career as a cop, evaporated like sea mist in the warm spring air.

I stood at the rear of the Volvo, hands on my hips, and surveyed the damage to my trunk and my bumper, minimal thanks to the Volvo being built like a tank but a major annoyance in my current frame of mind.

Two college-age kids climbed out of the SUV. The boy, sunburned with sun-streaked hair, was dressed in swim trunks and a Hawaiian shirt. His curvaceous dark-haired companion wore a bikini topped by a damp T-shirt, emblazoned with the Guess logo. From the generous size of her chest, I guessed implants.

My head was aching from the pounding my brain had taken from slamming into my skull at impact. I waved my arm at my dented bumper and damaged paint job and shouted, "What the hell were you doing? Don't you watch where you're going? Didn't you notice there was a car *and* a red light in front of you?"

Before I could ask if they had a cell phone to call the police, the boy's eyes widened.

"She's packing heat!" he screamed, and dived back through his open door. The girl ducked behind her side of the car.

When I'd moved my arm, my blazer had gaped open, and he'd caught sight of the gun in my shoulder holster. My yelling and angry expression had apparently triggered fears of road rage. But before I could calm his alarm, he popped out of his car again, holding a semiautomatic handgun and pointing it in my direction.

"Don't move, lady, or I'll blow you away."

From the slur in his voice, I could tell the driver had either been wasting away in Margaritaville early or had yet to sober up from the night before. Whichever the case, I was faced with an intoxicated idiot threatening me with a firearm.

"Put the gun down," I said in my most soothing voice and held my hands out at my sides in a nonintimidating posture, "or somebody's going to get hurt."

"Yeah, lady, and it's going to be you."

"Be reasonable. Why would you shoot me?"

"You've got a gun. You're mad as hell and could blow me away for smashing your car."

His girlfriend was talking on her cell phone on the other side of the SUV. I hoped she was calling 911 and not ordering pizza.

"If either of us uses deadly force," I tried to explain, "we'll be thrown in jail."

"Uh-huh." The slightly inebriated driver shook his head. "Not in Florida. There's a new law. If you threaten me, I can shoot you. No questions asked."

The kid was loosely interpreting the recent extension of the right to use deadly force, but the legalities at this point weren't pertinent. What mattered was his shaky grasp of the facts, his finger on the trigger and how quickly I could defuse the situation.

"I'm not threatening you," I assured him, keeping my voice low.

Although I'd like to wring his neck. My Volvo was old, but I'd bought it with money my father had left me, I'd spent a lot of hours both driving and on stakeout in that car, and it had great sentimental value.

"My gun's holstered," I said. "I'm a private investigator, a former cop. This is a simple accident. We exchange insurance information and go our separate ways. Looks like you're headed to the beach."

He kept the gun pointed in my general direction—he was too drunk to aim well—and he was either considering what I'd said or planning his best shot.

An approaching siren sounded in the distance, and I hoped the Clearwater PD had a cruiser on the way. As much as I didn't want to visit my mother, I'd rather not have a gunshot wound as an excuse to avoid her.

The siren's volume increased, and south of us, a police car turned the corner onto Fort Harrison and screeched to a stop behind the SUV.

"Put the gun down, kid," I warned, "before the cops shoot you."

"Do what she says, Richie," the girl called from behind the car.

Richie's bravado wavered along with his aim. Before the cop could exit his vehicle, Richie turned and stashed the gun beneath the seat of his SUV.

"Hey, Maggie," a familiar voice called out. Rudy

Beaton, a former Pelican Bay officer, had climbed out of the patrol car. He pushed back his cap and with a grin nodded toward the rear of my Volvo. "Looks like you got yourself a Signal Four here."

"And a Signal One," I said to alert Rudy to the drunken state of the driver.

Rudy surveyed the accident scene, then asked us to move our vehicles off busy Fort Harrison into an adjacent vacant parking lot. He parked his cruiser behind the SUV. Rudy's backup arrived, and the two administered a field sobriety test to the young driver, who failed miserably. The girl tested clean.

After the two cops had taken the pertinent information for the accident report, Rudy's backup placed Richie in the back seat of his cruiser and left for the short drive to the station.

Richie's girlfriend had tested sober, but she was a bundle of nerves after the incident.

"Can you drive?" Rudy asked her.

"Sure." She showed him her license, which she'd retrieved from her bag in the car.

"You sure you're okay?" he insisted.

The girl nodded again.

"You want to follow us to the station?" Rudy asked.

Another nod.

"Wish I could stay and catch up, Maggie," Rudy said to me, "but with spring break, we're busier than one-armed paperhangers."

"Be careful out there," I said.

"You, too." Rudy headed for his cruiser. The girl, still shaken from the accident, slid behind the wheel of the SUV. She fastened her seat belt, put the car into gear and stomped the gas.

The SUV lurched backward and smashed into the front of Rudy's patrol car, crumpling the hood.

I didn't know whether to laugh or cry.

I had waited while Rudy completed a second accident report, so it was afternoon when I reached the hospital.

Mother was sitting in a chair next to the window, and Caroline perched on the edge of the bed. When I entered the room, she hopped up, looking so incredibly cheerful, the polar opposite of my mood, that I felt an uncontrollable urge to slap her. Somehow I managed to grit my teeth and resist.

"Hi, Margaret. Mother, look who's here."

Mother shifted her gaze from the window to me.

Her mouth moved into a bizarre position, one side smiling, the other, still paralyzed from the stroke, frozen in a frown, her expression the perfect metaphor for the manner in which she'd treated me my entire life.

My head was still pounding from the accident, my hives were screaming, my nerves were frayed, my stomach grumbled with hunger, and I realized too late I should never have confronted my mother in my present state of mind.

"Hello, Mother. How are you feeling?"

"Terrible."

The word came out slowly and garbled, but the look in her eyes left no question what she'd meant. I had to give the old girl credit, though. In spite of her incapacitation, she was dressed in a soft blue peignoir with her hair neatly combed and her makeup artfully applied. Caroline's doing, I imagined.

Frazzled by the accident, I probably looked more like the one who'd had a stroke. I should have at least stopped in the restroom to comb my hair, which my mother was eyeing with her usual disdain.

"I'm sorry," I said to her, "that you've been through a rough time."

Caroline shifted to Mother's side, sat on the arm of the chair and placed her arm around Mother's shoulders. "Dr. Katz says she's making remarkable progress. She'll be going home in a day or so."

"That's good news." I forced myself to smile and wished that, in addition to my sympathy, I could muster some genuine warmth for the woman who'd borne me. "Is there anything I can do for you?"

Mother shook her head. She was obviously embarrassed by her inability to speak clearly, a condition that left her at a distinct disadvantage, since her sharp tongue and caustic words, albeit disguised in a genteel tone, had always been her best weapons.

As if to fill the void of silence, Caroline asked, "What have you been up to?"

I shrugged. "Just working."

Mother had never found criminal investigations suitable for conversation, so I provided no details.

Instead, I grabbed onto an appropriate social topic. "Bill and I plan to start house-hunting soon."

Caroline's interest quickened. "There's a house near us that just went on the market."

"Thanks. I'll tell Bill."

But even if we could afford the prices in Belle Terre,

such close proximity to both Mother and my sister was not a good idea. Neither had ever been touched by the crime and human suffering that had filled my life for so many years. Even without the added complication of Mother's inferiority complex and her resulting animosity toward me, I'd never be able to bridge the gap between us. Our worlds were too different. Living close to each other would never change that.

"I don't want to tire you, Mother, so I'd better be going." I approached her and kissed her papery cheek. I half expected her to jerk away, but she endured my feint at affection and made no attempt to reciprocate.

After a quick goodbye to Caroline, I hurried from the room. I'd paid the obligatory visit, but it had left me feeling unsettled and frustrated—and angry with myself for expecting more.

When I entered the office after a stop at Scallops for a turkey-stuffed croissant and iced tea with lime to go, Darcy, waving a white envelope, greeted me.

"Gracie Lattimore was in earlier. She left this for you. Said you'd requested it. She had a cute little dog with her."

My sleep-deprived brain took a moment to

process the information before I surmised that Gracie, at my suggestion, must have listed her demands to be met by Jolene before Gracie and Roger would return to the soap star's condo.

I carried the envelope and my takeout into my office and settled behind my desk. ·

After scarfing half my sandwich, I wiped my fingers on a paper napkin and slit open Gracie's envelope. The list, written in a round, childish script, was short:

1. Don't call me shithead.
2. Don't make fun of how I look.
3. Raise my salary.
4. Give me an extra day off a month.

Those four short sentences drew a pathetic picture of Gracie's existence in Jolene's employment and revealed as much about Gracie as the woman who'd hired her. Wishing Gracie had accepted the five thousand I'd offered and looked for another job, I dialed Jolene's cell phone.

When the soap star answered, I said, "This is Maggie Skerr—"

"I was just about to call you."

"Has something happened?"

Her throaty chuckle floated through the line. "Ah, yes. Something wonderful." Then her tone changed. "You don't have Roger, do you?"

"No, but—"

"Thank God."

"I thought you wanted him back." I was beginning to wonder if Jolene was operating on all cylinders.

"I do, but not yet."

"Not yet?" *What about poor little Roger's broken heart?*

"I'm off to Cancún for a while. I've met the most marvelous man. He owns a condo here in my building. I ran into him at the pool, and what that man does to a Speedo—but that's another story."

Already short on patience after a wrecked car and a visit with Mother, I asked, "What's this got to do with Roger?"

Jolene sighed, as if explaining to a mentally challenged child. "If I had Roger, I'd only have to board him until Ed and I get back from Mexico. While I'm away, the dog will be much happier with Gracie than in some strange kennel."

"But you still want the dog?"

"Eventually."

"Gracie has some demands before she'll give Roger back and return to work."

Jolene sighed again. "Gracie is always demanding. I'll deal with her when I return."

"What if she's found another job by then?" I knew Gracie wasn't looking, but I was hoping by implying otherwise to provide her some leverage with Jolene.

"Someone else hire Gracie?" Jolene snorted in disbelief. "You're kidding. You've met her, haven't you? Who'd hire Gracie?"

"You might be surprised."

Jolene's high-pitched laughter aggravated my headache. "You're right. I would be surprised. I'd be downright flabbergasted."

The woman was so annoying, I could understand why Gracie had left. What I couldn't understand was why she hadn't either poisoned Jolene's food or smothered her in her sleep before departing.

"So what should I tell Gracie?"

"Don't tell her anything," Jolene said with a hint of malice. "Let her sweat. I'll call you when I get back."

I groped for a zinger, but my whiplashed brain refused to cooperate.

"Bon voyage."

I consoled myself with thoughts of her $10,000 retainer and hung up.

CHAPTER 14

At the marina, Bill and I sat on the deck of the *Ten-Ninety-Eight* and watched the sun set over Caladesi Island, which had been named by the latest polls as number four of the nation's Top Ten Beaches. The sky at the horizon was the color of tangerines and mango pulp, and the warm breeze carried the briny scent of the gulf and a hint of Coppertone.

After a few sips of Bill's homemade sangria, a seductive concoction of burgundy, brandy and sliced lemons, limes and oranges, I felt the knots in my muscles, by-products of my tension-filled day, begin to loosen.

Salmon steaks sizzled on the grill along with yellow squash, onions and fresh asparagus. A tossed salad of fresh spinach, dried cranberries and chopped walnuts waited in the tiny galley fridge.

I lifted my glass to Bill in a toast and nodded toward the grill. "You're the only person I know who makes eating healthy appealing."

"Police work has taken a toll on our bodies," Bill said. "High stress, irregular hours with not enough sleep and too much fast food. Not to mention that we're not getting any younger. By eating healthy, we'll have a lot of years left to spend together."

His desire for a long married life touched me, but, as I'd done all my life, I hid my emotions behind a wisecrack. "Just don't cut off my doughnuts. I'll lose the will to live."

He grinned at my joke, one of the many things I loved about Malcolm.

Fortified by a few more swallows of sangria, I told Bill about my interview with Stella Branigan, my visit with Mother, the damage to my Volvo and my run-in with a drunken preppy gunslinger.

"The only good thing about the accident," I said, "was crossing paths with Rudy Beaton."

"You miss the guys at Pelican Bay."

I nodded. "Sometimes I even miss Chief Shelton."

"Do you know what he's doing now?"

"Retired. I ran into him a few days ago. He says

he plays golf every day. It's either that or stay at home where Myra makes him clean and vacuum."

"So his airheaded wife's a tyrant?"

I smiled. "What goes around, comes around."

Bill filled my glass with more sangria, then turned the salmon on the grill.

"Speaking of healthy eating and the Pelican Bay department," I said, "did I ever tell you how Steve Johnson used to season his microwaved burritos with department-issue pepper spray?"

Bill stared at me, his spatula suspended in midair. "You're kidding."

I shook my head. "And then he'd wonder why he had heartburn."

"Johnson never was particularly bright." Bill settled back into his deck chair and picked up his glass. "Is he still working for Home Depot in Clearwater?"

"Yep, in the paint section. Apparently they've learned to keep him away from sharp tools."

Over dinner on the deck, we discussed other former acquaintances and past experiences. Not until Bill had cleared the table and served coffee in thick mugs did we turn to business. By now, the sun had set and the crescent moon hung high in the sky. A scattering of brilliant stars were visible in spite of the ambient light from the marina.

"How did your workmen's comp case inquiry go today?" I asked.

"The investigation was over almost before I started," Bill said with a satisfied grin. "I went looking for a guy who supposedly injured his back lifting boxes of frozen chicken at the restaurant where he works. When I stopped at a convenience store to ask directions to his house, the clerk knew him. Told me this long story of how he was with the guy in his garage when he tried to winch the engine out of his Corvette and the chain slipped. The idiot grabbed at the chain to keep the engine from falling. Tore up his back something awful, the clerk said."

"Then decided to compound stupidity with fraud?"

Bill nodded. "At least I can close that case out quickly. You and I have being keeping busier than I intended, but it's hard to turn away clients before we're established well."

I stared into my coffee cup.

"Want to share what you're thinking?" Bill asked.

I shrugged. "What if I've got this Fisk/Branigan thing all wrong?"

"What do you mean?"

"I keep trying to make a connection, but maybe there isn't one. What if Deirdre used the picture from the newspaper as an excuse to go pub crawling without her sister? She could have hooked up with the wrong guy in some sleazy bar and ended up dead. And her murder had nothing to do with our cold case."

"And Branigan?"

"He was a politician, so he'd pissed off more people than you and I have ever met. Any one of them could have known where he lived, lain in wait for him in that arbor, and finished him off."

"Did you fax the cold-case DNA results to Doc?"

I nodded. "But she's backed up. Because it's not an active case—hell, it's not even in her jurisdiction—she has to put comparing it with Branigan's DNA at the bottom of her list. It could be a week or more before we know anything. Same with Archer Phillips and his info search." I laid my head along the back of the chair and studied the stars. "I've hit the wall in both investigations."

"Maybe you should consult a psychic."

I laughed. Bill knew I'd used that line to taunt my former chief whenever an investigation went dead in the water. Shelton had never risen to the bait, not because he didn't believe in such nonsense but because it would have cost the department too much money.

"I have a prediction." Bill stood, set my mug aside and pulled me to my feet.

"What does Swami Malcolm see in my future?"

"You're spending the night on a boat with a tall, dark man."

"Dark?"

"Well, suntanned, at least. But just because there's snow on the roof doesn't mean there's no fire in the furnace."

I couldn't resist teasing him. "You know what else they say?"

He tugged me closer. "What?"

"That by thirty-five you get your head together and your body starts falling apart."

"I don't feel a day over twenty," he said with an irresistible grin, "and I'd guess that you're just over eighteen."

"Why eighteen?"

"Because that makes what I have in mind legal."

He kissed me then, and all thoughts of murders and cold cases disappeared.

The next morning, Bill and I met with Adler at the Clearwater PD. Although it was Saturday, both he and Porter had come in early. With two active homicide investigations, they'd have no days off until they'd either solved the cases or reached dead ends.

The office was an interior room with no windows, a dropped ceiling and bad fluorescent lighting. In those drab surroundings, the occupants were unaware of the glorious day outside filled with brilliant sunshine, warm breezes and wall-to-wall college kids.

Just the thought of college kids made my head and neck ache, and I wondered if Richie the Gunslinger was still incarcerated in a nearby holding cell or if his bumper-car girlfriend had sprung for his bail.

Adler, as always, was eating. His breakfast of choice, spread across the top of his desk, was an Egg McMuffin, a plate-sized cinnamon bun and coffee.

Porter was sprinkling wheat germ into a carton of low-fat yogurt. They invited us to help ourselves to coffee from the pot in the break room. We took them up on the offer, then settled down to business.

"We've turned up squat on Fisk's killer," Adler said between bites.

"Maggie's had some luck," Bill said.

"Great," Porter drawled. "We could use a break."

"I don't know how helpful it is." I told them about the young hooker I'd interviewed in the park and gave them her description of the perp. "We've already eliminated the men in the *Tribune* photo, so there's no evidence to tie Deirdre's murder to Branigan's."

"Got a theory?" Adler asked.

I shrugged. "Just a shot in the dark. Maybe Deirdre wasn't the shy, retiring woman her sister claims. After all, they'd lived in different states for years. What if Deirdre had a dark side—a result of her earlier molestation—that had her prowling bars, looking for Mr. Goodbar?"

"And she found him?" Porter asked.

"Who else would it be?" Bill said. "According to the witness, Deirdre recognized her assailant, even ran to meet him."

Adler frowned. "If that scenario pans out, we have a killer loose who might strike again. You think this hooker could come up with a full description?"

I hesitated, filled with the irrational hope that the kid could clean up her act and avoid all contact with the police. But with lives at stake, I had no choice. "She works the park bench just west of where Deirdre's body was found. Maybe she'll be there tonight. But she said the guy was wearing a hat and sunglasses—"

"So did the Unabomber," Adler said.

But the Unabomber sketch hadn't been the key to his capture, I thought, but kept it to myself.

"I'll have a uniform pick her up tonight," Adler said, "and put her with a sketch artist. Then we'll canvass area bars with the description, even ask the local TV stations to air it."

Porter noisily scraped the last bit of yogurt from the cup with a plastic spoon, licked it and tossed the spoon and container into his wastebasket. "Which brings us to the Branigan case."

"We're coming up empty there, too," Adler said. "We checked out the guy in Safety Harbor who wrote threatening letters to Branigan after losing his job due to legislation Branigan sponsored—"

"And the Hispanic day laborer," Porter added, "the one who made threats because of Branigan's lack of support for migrant workers."

"Both have rock-solid alibis," Adler said.

"What about the feminist in Belleair?" Bill asked.

"Georgia Harding?" Adler rolled his eyes. "She's something else. Wouldn't even let us in the door. A real man-hater." His expression brightened. "Maybe she'll talk to you, Maggie."

I almost choked on my coffee. "Why me? Some of my best friends are men."

Bill looked thoughtful. "Adler's right. You've succeeded in a male-dominated career. Maybe she'll be more open to you."

"Okay," I said, "why not? I can bill my time to Mrs. Branigan, since she's hired me to investigate. I'll check out Georgia Harding after the funeral this afternoon. Will you two be there?"

Adler nodded. "We'll attend the service at the church and the gathering afterward at the Branigan house."

"Watch out for Sidney and his wife," I said. "There's tension in that family."

Porter snorted. "There's tension in every family.

Especially after a death. Where there's a will, there's a relative."

"Who gets Branigan's estate?" I asked.

"What estate?" Adler had finished his sandwich and worked his way through half his cinnamon bun. "The wife has all the money. Branigan was financially dependent on her."

"So we can rule out greed as a motive," Bill said.

"And the wife as a suspect," Porter said. "Both the cleaning woman and the butler place her in her room at the time of the murder."

"Two witnesses whose salaries she pays," I observed.

"You suggesting they were bribed?" Adler said.

"Been known to happen," I said.

"But if she has all the money," Bill said, "what's her motive?"

I thought of Archer Phillips and his secret love nest. "Could Branigan have had a little action going on the side? Some women are drawn to powerful men."

"As well as to jocks and rock stars," Porter said with a sigh. "Life ain't fair."

"If life was fair," I said, "we'd all be out of a job."

"And if you had women throwing themselves at you," Adler told Porter, "your wife would kill you."

"But what a way to go," Porter shot back.

Adler finished his bun and coffee and seemed to be looking around for something else to consume. "We already checked the cheating-husband angle with Branigan's aides. They swear he was squeaky clean. He may have been interested in fooling around, but he was terrified his political enemies would find out—"

"And use it against him?" I asked.

Adler shook his head. "And tell his wife. Apparently Branigan had a healthy respect for Stella."

"And her bank accounts," Porter added.

Frustrated by lack of progress, I stood to leave. The only solid results of our investigation were the new hives that had risen on my arms. Bill promised we'd all meet to compare notes after the funeral and my interview with Georgia Harding and followed me out the door.

CHAPTER 15

Carlton Branigan's memorial service was held at two o'clock at Peace Memorial Presbyterian Church in downtown Clearwater. The public service followed a private burial at Sylvan Abbey.

Dwarfed by its neighbor, a former resort hotel that now served as World Headquarters for the Church of Scientology, pink-stuccoed Peace, like many historic Florida churches, had been built in a Spanish mission style. With heavy wooden doors, a roof of sunbaked clay tiles, seventy stained-glass windows, including two massive creations by Louis Comfort Tiffany, and a soaring belfry topped by an ornate wrought-iron cross, the sanctuary had been erected after World War I. William Jennings Bryan had spoken at its dedication to those who'd died in the Great War.

Today the church was again filled with dignitaries, including the governor and his wife, whom ushers seated just before Stella, accompanied by Sidney and Angela, was escorted down the aisle to a front pew.

Stella and Angela were attired in black designer dresses with stylish hats whose black, ribbon-edged veils obscured their faces. Sidney, wearing a shell-shocked expression and a navy-blue suit, sat between his wife and mother. Brianna was nowhere in sight. I would try to talk to her at her home while her parents were at the reception at Stella's following the funeral.

Bill and I slipped into a pew at the rear of the church, and I caught a glimpse of Adler and Porter seated opposite us across the center aisle. The sanctuary was packed with the powerful, the rich and the famous from around the city and the state, and, outside the church, cordons of uniformed officers, supplemented by sheriff's deputies, held the media and the curious at bay. Unknown to the crowd, Adler had arranged for a CSU tech, disguised as a news photographer, to snap pictures of the attendees. If a malcontent voter had killed Branigan, his appearance at the funeral was a distinct possibility, and he might be spotted in the photos.

Inside, the organist completed Samuel Barber's *Adagio*, and the opening strains of a familiar hymn soared from the Casavant pipe organ. Everyone rose to sing, but Bill and I paid more attention to the congregation than to the elaborately choreographed service as we watched for anyone who looked suspicious or out of place.

In addition to the minister's homily, eulogies were delivered by everyone from the governor to the mayor. I kept expecting Sidney to pay some tribute to his father, but he remained at his mother's side throughout the service. If I believed everything that was said about the late senator, he'd been a saint and a hero, incapable of any wrongdoing, much less molesting and murdering children.

When the service ended, Bill and I hurried outside and conducted our own surveillance of the crowd. Many appeared to be college kids, caught in the traffic jam and making the most of an opportunity to see celebrities. Others, dressed in the military-style uniforms of the Church of Scientology, had obviously been trapped by the crush of people around the church. Several typical tourists, a few vagrants and possibly some folks who worked in nearby offices, gawked at the governor and other famous faces, but no one stood out as a potential suspect. Adler would study the photos taken by the crime-scene tech later and have a few run through face recognition software to search for matches with known criminals.

Attendants from the funeral home scuttled the Branigan family out a side door into a waiting limousine that drove quickly away. Bill and I walked through an alley behind the church to the next street over where he'd parked his SUV.

"That was an exercise in futility," he complained.

"Our job would be so much easier if someone had just gotten up, gone to the lectern and admitted, 'I killed him and I'm glad.'"

Bill unlocked the car doors and opened mine. "If Branigan was as great as everyone proclaimed, how come somebody strangled him?"

"Obviously—" I fastened my seat belt "—we're missing something. I found it interesting that Sidney didn't speak at the service."

"Maybe he was afraid. Speaking in public is the number-two phobia, after all."

"And you know this how?" Bill continually amazed me with the factoids he could pull from thin air.

"Discovery Channel." He closed my door, circled the car and climbed into the driver's seat.

"What's the number-one phobia?" I asked.

"Fear of spiders. And did you know that one in ten people experience a phobia at sometime in their lives?" He started the engine, checked the lane behind him and pulled away from the curb.

"Not me," I insisted.

"Yeah, I know." He pointed to my face. "You're allergic, not phobic."

I popped another Benadryl. "This allergy started with the child murders. If we can solve them, maybe my hives will go away for good."

"You still think Branigan's a suspect?" Bill had circled the block and headed south toward Harbor Oaks.

"It's a long shot. Doc's DNA comparisons will tell us more."

"According to the files," Bill said, "Mackley had the killer's DNA sample run through every available data bank just last year and came up empty.

Whoever our guy is, he's not a registered sex of-
fender."

Frustration made my skin itch. I'd been trying to
connect the cold cases with the Fisk and Branigan
murders without success. And, unless we had a break
in one of the homicides soon, they'd all be cold.

The street in front of the Branigan house was
clogged with parked cars by the time we arrived. Bill
had to leave his SUV three blocks away, and I was
glad for the cooling sea breeze as we walked to the
reception. The trek in pumps with two-inch heels
that matched my navy dress and jacket, formerly
reserved for court appearances, killed my feet. I
hoped my nondescript attire, an unassuming outfit
that made Caroline shudder at its plainness, would
help me blend into the crowd of guests streaming
into the Branigan home.

Madison frowned at us when we entered the
house but made no effort to stop us, probably because
he didn't want to cause a scene in front of so many
important guests. We passed through the entry hall
to the rear terrace, where an elaborate buffet had
been set up by the caterers. Round dining tables,
covered with ivory-colored linens and centered with

massive arrangements of cream-colored roses and orchids, had been scattered across the rolling lawn and around the pool. Some guests had already filled their plates and taken seats. Others chatted in small groups but kept their conversations muted.

"We'll cover more ground if we split up," Bill said.

I nodded. "When this is over, I'll meet you at the car."

Bill moved away into the crowd, and I couldn't help noting that, in his well-cut suit, he looked as distinguished as any of the movers and shakers.

I went through the buffet line and placed a couple of finger sandwiches on my plate while I eavesdropped on the people nearby.

"Carlton's death was *so* horrible," one elegantly dressed woman was saying to her companion. "It's one thing to die peacefully in your sleep, but murdered in your own backyard?"

"Too much crime in today's world," her dapper escort complained. "I'll bet you when they catch whoever did it, he's an illegal alien."

"What makes you say that?" she asked.

He looked astounded. "Don't you watch Fox News? Murders by illegal aliens are happening all over the country. And they'll continue until we clamp down on the borders."

Plate in hand, I moved away. After finding a wrought-iron bench beneath a ligustrum tree, I sat, rested my aching feet and surveyed the crowd. Stella, looking pale but stoic, moved among her guests, shaking hands, having her cheek kissed and accepting condolences. Angela and Sidney had taken seats at a table by the pool, where Sidney glared into his drink. Occasionally someone would stop, place a hand on Sidney's shoulder, and speak briefly, but the son's prickly attitude discouraged further conversation.

People avoided the arbor where Carlton had died. Someone, perhaps Madison or the caterers, had placed two massive palms in jardinieres and a bamboo screen in front of the entrance, either to discourage the curious or to spare Stella from having to look at her husband's murder scene all afternoon.

Anyone who used the buffet table had to walk past my bench to reach the lawn, and, although I kept my eyes and ears open, I neither saw nor heard anything helpful to the investigation of Carlton's murder. I caught sight of Bill at the far end of the pool, still working the crowd, and I decided to slip next door.

No one seemed to notice as I sauntered toward the break in the hedge and took the path that led into Sidney's property. On the other side of his garage, a delicate-looking child with long blond hair and blue eyes and dressed in shorts, a T-shirt and sneakers, was sitting in a swing beneath a live oak. She looked startled when she spotted me.

"It's okay, Brianna," I said. "I work for your grandmother."

She braced her feet against the ground to stop the swing and looked ready to bolt for the house. "I'm not supposed to talk to strangers."

"That's a good rule," I said. "Why don't you go find Ingrid? She knows me. We'll see if Ingrid says it's okay for us to talk."

I backed away to give her space, and she raced toward the back door. She reappeared a moment later with Ingrid in tow.

"Ms. Skerritt," Ingrid said with obvious relief when she recognized me. "Brianna said there was a stranger in the yard."

"I hope you don't mind," I said. "I'm escaping from the crush next door. I could barely breathe in that crowd."

Ingrid nodded. The buzz of hundreds of voices carried over the hedge.

"Is it okay if I stay here a moment and catch my breath?"

She looked hesitant. "I suppose it's all right. I have packing to finish."

"You're taking a trip?"

"Not me. The Branigans. They're leaving for the Caribbean Monday morning."

"Don't let me take you from your work," I said. "Maybe Brianna will keep me company."

Brianna, in a burst of shyness, grabbed the house-keeper's hand.

"It's okay, sweetheart," Ingrid said. "Ms. Skerritt is a nice lady, and she used to be a policewoman."

"Really?" Brianna seemed impressed and released Ingrid to study me closer.

"Really." I nodded to Ingrid, and she turned to head back inside.

"Did you ever shoot anybody?" Brianna asked.

Memories of my first months on the job, when I'd been Malcolm's partner, flashed through my mind. We'd answered a domestic-abuse call. The battered and terrified wife had grabbed Bill, and her coke-crazed husband had attacked him with a machete. I'd fired three rounds into the husband's chest, killing him almost instantly. My quick action had earned Bill's gratitude and respect and erased his objections to having a woman partner. The rest, as they say, is history.

But I sidestepped Brianna's question about shootings, figuring she'd had enough violence in her young life the past few days. "Cops don't like to use their guns. We prefer to settle things peacefully."

"Oh." She returned to her swing, and I moved to a lawn chair within conversation range.

"What else do cops do?" Brianna asked.

She'd given me the opening I'd hoped for. "They arrest bad people. Do you know any bad people?"

She didn't answer and stared at her feet, then pushed off until her swing formed a high arc.

I watched her swing for a few minutes. When she slowed down, I said, "I'm sorry about your grandfather."

I didn't know how much her parents had told her, but I was fairly certain the child knew that Carlton was dead.

She planted her feet, stopped the swing and cocked her head. "He won't ever be coming back?"

Her voice and expression were devoid of emotion, and I didn't try to answer her with tales of heaven and the Great Beyond. If Carlton had done what I suspected, he was roasting on a spit in hell. "No, he won't be coming back."

She nodded, but her features remained expressionless and gave no clue to her feelings about her grandfather. She glanced past me toward her grandparents' house, and her face brightened.

"Hi, Daddy."

I turned and saw Sidney approaching. His face was florid with anger and possibly too much drink.

Before he could speak, I held up my hands. "I was just leaving."

"Not fast enough," he said with a snarl.

I wiggled my fingers at the little girl. "Bye, Brianna. Enjoy your vacation."

I hurried past Sidney and through the gap in the hedge, then plunged into the crowd still gathered next door. Within minutes, I found Bill by the buffet table, chatting with Edward Raleigh, the state senator from Pelican Bay, and his wife.

Several dozen inane conversations later, I waited out front for Bill to pick me up. After observing my limp from the high heels I was unaccustomed to wearing, he offered to go after the car and spare me the three-block hike. God, I loved that man.

CHAPTER 16

Bill dropped me off at my condo, and I changed clothes as well as shoes. For my interview with Georgia Harding, I scrubbed off my minimal makeup and donned sneakers, jeans and a T-shirt that read Grow Your Own Dope—Plant a Man. Darcy had given it to me as a joke several Christmases ago, and I was hoping the message would strike a chord with the self-proclaimed feminist and make her more willing to talk.

I climbed into my Volvo, battered but still functional after its rear-end collision, and drove south through Clearwater. Belleair was nestled between Clearwater and Largo, and the section along the waterfront was home to millionaires and movie stars, including wrestler Hulk Hogan. On the other side of what used to be the tracks but was now the Pinellas Trail, a linear park that bisected the county, were more modest houses. That's where I found Georgia Harding's cement-block cottage. From the overgrown state of her yard and the disrepair of her house, Georgia needed to find herself a good man, or, at least, to hire one who knew how to use a lawn mower, power tools and a paintbrush.

I knocked on a jalousie pane of the front door. Georgia must have heard my car and been watching, because the door opened immediately. I was expecting a radical feminist, and I wasn't disappointed. Sans makeup, Georgia wore men's slacks, a loose-fitting tie-dyed shirt that didn't quite hide the absence of a bra, and an attitude. She looked about as approachable as a porcupine. John Lennon glasses perched on her prominent nose, and her long frizzy hair exploded around her face like a brown nimbus streaked with gray. According to the data Adler had pulled from her driver's license, she was sixty-two. Her frown softened only slightly when she read the slogan on my shirt.

I introduced myself and gave her my card. "I'm here to talk about Carlton Branigan."

"That jerk? He's dead." And she wasn't exactly broken up about it.

"Unfortunately," I said, "not from natural causes."

She appeared ready to slam the door in my face, so I continued quickly. "Here's the deal. You can either answer my questions now or talk to the cops later when they haul you into the station. Your call."

With a sigh of resignation, she stood aside. I stepped into what in most homes would have been a living room, but hers was command central. Instead of framed art, the walls sported posters of everything from Greenpeace, NOW and Tampa Bay Gay and Lesbian Pride to a picture of Karl Marx. In the middle of the room was a desk topped with a computer, fax machine and printer and surrounded by eight-foot tables piled high with bundles of leaflets and flyers. Cardboard posters, lettered with typical antiestablishment slogans, and, surprisingly, a few that read Save The Belleview Biltmore, a historic Belleair resort, were propped in the room's corners. Except for a few paper clips, rubber bands and a litter of dust bunnies, the terrazo floor was bare.

Georgia removed a stack of folders from a metal

chair and offered me a seat. Even in sneakers, my feet still hurt, so I took it.

She sat behind her desk and peered at me with a hostile expression over the frames of her glasses. "So you're a private eye?"

I nodded. "Mrs. Branigan hired me to investigate her husband's murder."

Her lip curled in a sneer. "I thought that was the pigs' job."

I couldn't ignore the insult. "I was a cop myself for more than twenty years."

Picturing a much younger Georgia during the Vietnam era, carrying a sign that read Hell, No, We Won't Go! or Make Love, Not War, and being hauled away from a demonstration by baton-wielding uniforms in riot gear, I added, "Cops aren't always the bad guys."

"Fascist pigs," Georgia muttered with a grunt of disgust. The woman was obviously enraged at a world she couldn't control. "Male Oppressors."

"Hold that thought," I said. "Maybe it will keep you from dialing 911 if someone tries to break into your house. Or steals your car. Or an antifeminist whacko with a gun and half a brain is stalking you."

Two unsolved homicides and the annoying spat between Jolene and Gracie had my nerves inflamed and my temper on a short fuse. I refused to sit quietly while Georgia denigrated my life's work and the men and women who put their lives on the line every day.

Georgia leaned back in her chair and glared at me for a moment. Then, unexpectedly, she relaxed, and her face broke into a broad smile that made her almost pretty. "I like you. I bet you don't take crap off anyone."

"I had a special course at the police academy," I said. "Crap Deflection 101."

And my take-no-nonsense attitude usually worked, with almost everyone except my mother. I realized with a sinking feeling that I hadn't checked on her today. Caroline would have called if Mother had taken a turn for the worse, so it wasn't Mother's health I worried about but the fallout from neglecting her.

And Georgia thought *cops* were oppressors. She'd never met Priscilla Skerritt.

"So why are you—and the police—interested in me?" Georgia's disdain had lessened, and she seemed less on guard.

"Your hate mail to Senator Branigan is on file at his office."

"Hate mail?" Georgia snorted. "I only wrote the truth. Are you aware of that man's abysmal voting record?"

"No." But I was sure she was going to tell me.

"He's anti-everything. Women's rights, gay marriage, abortion, preserving the environment. You name it, he's against it. If he had his way, women would still be without the vote and eternally barefoot and pregnant." Hatred contorted her features, and her strong, lean fingers clenched in anger.

"You sound passionate," I said. "It took someone with a lot of passion and a ton of rage to strangle Branigan to death."

She shook her head. "I didn't kill him, but I'm not sorry he's dead."

"Where were you Wednesday morning?"

"Picketing outside MacDill Airbase in Tampa. The vice president was visiting CentCom. A few of my friends and I gave him a welcoming party."

"Can anyone verify that?"

"Yeah, Channel 8. Their crews took miles of film footage. We made the noon and evening news and the metro section of Thursday's *Tribune*. In fact—" she swung her desk chair toward her computer and hit a few keys, then swiveled her laptop so I could see the display screen "—I'm there, on the right."

She had accessed the *Tribune*'s archives, and her face stared back at me from the photo of a group of protestors taken Wednesday morning, according to the caption.

Her alibi eliminated her as Branigan's killer but upped my frustration level. The feminist had been our last named suspect. Now the Clearwater cops and Bill and I were operating in the dark in our search for the murderer. We had no further suspects, no motives, and too many days since the murder. The trail was getting colder by the minute.

"That's all I needed to know." I pushed to my feet. "Thanks for your time."

Georgia walked me to the door and, as I was leaving, nodded toward the wording on my shirt. "Are you a feminist?"

I thought of the lawsuit I'd filed and won fifteen years ago, when Chief Shelton had refused to hire me for the Pelican Bay Police Department because I was female. "Yes, I suppose I am."

Georgia grinned, and I added quickly, "But I'm not giving up my bra."

* * *

Gracie Lattimore's uncle's house was only a few miles south of Georgia Harding's, so I decided to pay Gracie a call while I was near the neighborhood. In less than ten minutes after leaving Georgia, I was parking in front of the Largo bungalow.

The sun was setting as I went up the front walk, and cooking odors assaulted me when Gracie opened the front door.

So did Roger. His enthusiastic coupling with my leg left no doubt that he was delighted to see me.

Gracie grabbed him by the collar and reined him in. "Bad boy, Roger. It's a good thing Jolene had you fixed, or no telling how you'd behave."

Roger, however, appeared unrepentant. He strained at his collar and grinned at me, his tail wagging so hard his entire hind end gyrated.

"I don't want to interrupt your meal," I said to Gracie.

"I'm finished. Except for the cleaning up. Have you talked to Jolene?"

I nodded. "That's why I'm here."

To my surprise, Gracie appeared disappointed. "Have a seat, please, and tell me what she said."

The Lattimores' living room was tiny and threadbare, the furniture topped with crocheted doilies and knickknacks, and every surface so clean it sparkled. I sat on a sofa and Gracie settled into an oversize recliner. Roger hopped onto the sofa beside me, turned around three times and stretched out against my thigh with a happy grunt.

Except for the ticking of a clock on the fireplace mantel and Roger's snuffles, the house was quiet.

"Are your aunt and uncle home?" I asked.

"Uncle Slim and Aunt Ruth are traveling with Uncle Frank. Roger and I have the whole house to ourselves. It's great, isn't it, Rog?"

Roger, who was now asleep, didn't answer.

I told Gracie about Jolene's phone call and her whirlwind trip to Cancún. "So I won't be able to give her your demands until she returns."

"Good," Gracie said with a satisfied nod.

"Good? Don't you need your job back?" With both Gracie and her boss, I could never figure out what they really wanted.

"I'll get my job back." Gracie folded her hands in her lap and smiled.

I didn't share her optimism. "I'll present your

demands to Jolene when she returns, but I can't guarantee she'll agree to them."

Gracie's smile widened, and her eyes shone behind her wire-rimmed glasses. "She'll agree."

Apparently Gracie knew something I didn't or she'd had too much happy juice with her dinner. "How can you be so sure?"

"Because I'm writing a book. All this peace and quiet has given me plenty of time to think. And work."

"A book?" Did Gracie really think she could support herself by writing? As a former librarian, I knew how few writers earned a decent living without keeping their day jobs.

"It's a tell-all exposé," she said. "I'm calling it *Heartbeats: Thirty Years Behind the Scenes*. I got to thinking about what skills I've learned from working with Jolene, and it hit me. I don't need skills. I know where all the bodies are buried."

"Dishing dirt can get you sued."

"Oh, I don't intend to publish it. Just put it into a safety-deposit box as insurance."

Beside me, Roger woofed softly, rolled onto his side and kneaded my thigh with all four feet, chasing rabbits in his sleep.

"When you give Jolene my demands," Gracie said, looking pleased with herself, "you can mention the book."

"That's blackmail," I said. "She could have you arrested."

Gracie shook her head. "Worst move she could make. Think of the publicity—and the interest in the book—my arrest would cause."

Gracie had a point, but I didn't relish being the one to break the news of her book to Jolene. I consoled myself with thoughts of Jolene's hefty retainer, promised to contact Gracie after I'd spoken with Jolene upon her return from Cancún, and left.

On the drive home, I laughed out loud. Jolene was in for a surprise. Given time to herself, mousy little Gracie had grown a backbone.

And big teeth.

CHAPTER 17

Sunday morning, with two murder investigations dead in the water, I enjoyed the rare luxury of a leisurely breakfast on my patio. Over coffee and frozen muffins nuked in the microwave, I read the *Times* and watched the comical brown pelicans for which my town was named divebomb for fish in St. Joseph Sound. An endless line of boats streamed through the channel, headed for deep-sea fishing or a day on Caladesi's famous beaches.

My morning destination was less alluring. As soon as I'd given her time for breakfast and a round with her doctor, I'd head to the hospital for a visit with Mother. Knowing that I'd sooner have a root canal filled me with guilt, until I remembered Seton Fellows's revelations. My mother and her insecurities were responsible for the uneasy state of our relationship, not me. As long as I could hold on to that fact—or until I came face-to-face with her—I refused to let her intimidate me.

But, as always, Mother kept me off balance. I arrived at her hospital room to find that she'd been released just minutes earlier. Determined to be the good daughter, I drove to her house.

Estelle answered the door. "Your mama's done gone to sleep. She's glad to be back in her own bed."

"She climbed the stairs?"

"Wouldn't hear of sleeping in the guest room, no matter how hard Miss Caroline begged."

"Is Caroline here?"

Estelle nodded. "Having coffee in the kitchen. Come in. I'll pour you a cup."

I stepped inside and followed Estelle down the hall.

Caroline looked up with surprise when I entered the kitchen. "What are you doing here?"

"I must have just missed you at the hospital. Thanks for telling me Mother was checking out."

"Sorry. I didn't know it myself until Dr. Katz made his rounds. Mother insisted on coming home. Said he couldn't keep her against her will." Caroline shrugged. "You know Mother."

Although Caroline was impeccably dressed in navy slacks and a white pullover and her makeup was perfection, her smart clothes couldn't hide the weary slump of her shoulders, and her expensive powders and creams didn't conceal the shadows under her eyes. I felt a twinge of remorse at having left Mother's care to my sister, even though I knew that's what Mother had preferred.

"Anything I can do to help here?" I hoped to be assigned a task that would assuage my guilt and took the mug of coffee Estelle had poured for me.

Caroline shook her head. "I ordered a hospital bed for the guest room, but it looks as if I'll have to cancel that. Mother insists on using her own room and resuming her normal routine."

"Is that safe?" I asked.

"Safer than getting her dander up," Estelle said with a grunt. "Ain't nobody on this earth able to say no to Miz Skerritt."

"You've got that right," Caroline agreed, and her voice reflected her fatigue.

"Go home," I told her. "I'll stay here today in case Mother needs something."

Caroline cast me a grateful glance, pushed back from the table and stood. "She'll probably sleep for hours. She complained that with all the noise and poking and prodding, she didn't sleep a wink during her stay at the hospital."

"I can handle Miz Skerritt," Estelle said. "No need for you girls to hang around here, twiddling your thumbs."

Caroline looked at me and shrugged. "She's right. But staying is up to you. If you don't have anything better to do—"

"I could come back later," I said, "when she's awake."

But I wasn't sure how much of my company, if any, Mother wanted.

"How 'bout I call if she needs you?" Estelle said.

"Good idea," I said, and, feeling like an escaping felon, I fled to my car.

Two messages were waiting on my answering machine. The first was from Adler, wanting me to call him at home. I was glad to hear that he was spending Sunday morning with his family. He'd been working at the station when I'd talked with him last night to report on the futility of my interview with Georgia Harding. I hoped his latest message meant he'd turned up another lead, so I returned his call.

"Anything new?" I asked when he answered the phone.

"Yeah, we picked up that young hooker in the park last night, and she worked with the sketch artist. Porter and I will start hitting the bars around Crest Lake with the sketches after lunch. Maybe we'll get lucky and someone will ID Fisk's killer."

"Take Deirdre's photo, too. Maybe someone saw them together." Bill and I had already shown Deirdre's picture to employees at bars and restaurants around Crest Lake Park, but no one had recognized her. Maybe with Deirdre's face paired with the sketch of her killer, Adler would get a lucky break.

"Already thought of that," Adler said, but in an easy manner that indicated no offense at my meddling.

"What about the hooker? Was she charged?" I'd thought often of the young girl since encountering her on the park bench and wondered if she'd survive the life she'd chosen.

"No, but Mary Garrabrant, one of our detectives who's good with young people, talked her into entering a shelter for abused women. The kid is terrified of her pimp, but she'll be safe there. With some help, maybe she'll straighten herself out."

"Good. Let me know if you get a hit on the sketches. Better yet, call Malcolm on his cell phone."

My second message was from Bill. "Call me when you get in."

I looked at my watch. It was after eleven. Maybe he wanted to take me to lunch.

"We have an appointment," he said when I reached him.

"An interview? There's no one left to interrogate."

"This is pleasure, not business."

The sound of his voice, rich and deep, eased my nerves and lessened the itching from my hives, stirred up by my near-visit with Mother.

"What kind of appointment? Reservations for lunch?" I could always hope.

"I'll take you to lunch after. Maybe we'll have something to celebrate."

"After what?"

"It's a surprise. There's walking involved. Wear comfortable shoes."

"I don't own any other kind." Except the heels I'd worn to the funeral and one pair of torturous stilettos that Caroline had made me buy last year for a Christmas tea. I would have donated the latter to Goodwill but feared ruining the feet of someone who couldn't afford a podiatrist, so they remained hidden in the back of my closet.

"I'll pick you up at one. Love you." And with a loud kissy sound, Bill hung up.

Bill arrived promptly at one, and I climbed into his SUV with trepidation. The last time he'd surprised me, he'd harnessed a flock of eight prancing plywood flamingos to his cabin cruiser for the Christmas boat parade. I was reluctant to imagine what he had planned for this afternoon.

After kissing me with his usual enthusiasm, he put the car in gear and pressed the gas. Within minutes, he was turning into Adler's neighborhood.

"Are we visiting Dave and Sharon?" I asked.

Bill shook his head. "We're meeting Natalie Pettigrew."

"Who's she?"

He grinned and patted my hand. "You'll see."

He went past the Adler house, turned a corner and drove two more blocks before pulling to the curb and turning off the engine.

"We're here," he announced.

I looked around at the attractive homes, grassy lawns, and huge shade trees that sheltered the street from the blazing April sun.

"The question," I said, "is why?"

He pointed to the house directly across from the SUV. "We're house-hunting."

Only then did I notice the Realtor's sign in the front yard that prominently displayed Natalie Pettigrew's name, face and phone number.

A plethora of emotions hit me, including surprise, curiosity and an overwhelming urge to jump from the car and run.

Bill grabbed my hand. "Relax. We're only looking. And that doesn't obligate us. If it helps, just think of the house as a crime scene and see what it tells you."

"A crime scene? You've got to be kidding."

His laugh and the twinkle in his blue eyes assured me he was.

The house, a Cape Cod with high gables and a steeply pitched roof, had been built in the forties. With its sage clapboard siding, roof of flat white tiles, and white shutters at the windows, the place needed only a white picket fence to match a *Leave It to Beaver* set.

"What do you think?" Bill asked.

"If you expect me to live in this June Cleaver environment, I'll need pearls and an apron."

His smile faded, and I immediately regretted bursting his bubble.

"It's lovely," I hastened to add. "It has *home* written all over it."

Bill's good humor returned. "You said a few days ago that you wouldn't mind looking at houses in this neighborhood, remember?"

But I hadn't expected Bill to start our house search so soon. Status quo was my natural condition, and the prospect of moving from my familiar condo filled me with anxiety. For Bill's sake, however, I'd keep my reservations to myself.

A dark blue BMW parked behind us. A young woman with bouffant strawberry-blond hair got out and approached the SUV. She was wearing a navy sleeveless dress, matching high heels and a beauty-contestant smile, and carrying an attaché case.

"That must be Natalie." Bill opened his door. "Now we can see inside."

His excitement was infectious. I left the car and, after meeting Natalie, accompanied Bill up the front walk. Tall crepe myrtle trees on either side of the entrance were just leafing out, and beds of flowering perennials and Indian hawthorn surrounded the house's foundation.

Before going inside, I glanced at the nearby houses. All were well maintained with attractive yards. And the street was tranquil and deserted, even on a Sunday afternoon.

Natalie fiddled with the lockbox on the paneled burgundy-red front door, then opened it with a flourish. "Y'all just go on in, make yourselves at home, and take a look. You'll find everything remodeled and updated. The house is empty, so y'all won't disturb anyone."

Judging by the slow cadence of her speech, Natalie was definitely from somewhere in the Deep South. Folks like me, who'd grown up in Pelican Bay, had a polyglot accent, a mixture of Midwest and

New England with a liberal dose of Southernisms, a linguistic gumbo.

But thoughts of dialects disappeared when I stepped into the bare but sunny living room. Four tall sash windows flooded the spacious room and high ceiling with light that shimmered on the polished heart pine floors. Built-in bookcases, perfect for all the books I hadn't had time to read, filled one wall, and a fireplace with an oak mantel another.

"This house is deceiving," Natalie said. "It looks small from the street. Follow me."

In the adjoining dining room, we saw what she meant. The house was built in a U-formation with French doors that opened from all the rooms onto a shaded courtyard, where a brick patio surrounded a weeping Chinese elm. Beds filled with pink and green caladiums, white pentas, Indian hawthorn, and nandina edged the brick seating area, and a fence across the back of the courtyard created a private, tranquil oasis. Not a water view like my condo had, but impressive.

"Wow!"

I followed the sound of Bill's voice and found him

in the kitchen. His expression was the same he'd worn when he first laid eyes on the *Ten-Ninety-Eight*. Bill had fallen in love.

"Look at this place." Awe tinged his voice. "Stainless-steel appliances, maple Shaker cabinets, slate floors, miles of granite countertops, a breakfast nook with built-in banquettes, and all with a view of that fabulous courtyard through a wall of French doors."

"It's definitely bigger than your galley," I said.

"With a kitchen like this, I might never eat out again."

I looked around for Natalie, but she had disappeared into another part of the house, apparently to give us privacy to explore on our own.

"We haven't seen the bedrooms and baths," I said. "Don't make your mind up yet."

With reluctance, Bill left the kitchen, and we continued the tour. The front bedroom was small, but perfect for an office, and there was a tiny but updated full bath off the hall. The master suite, however, was huge, with a big bedroom, a sitting room, two walk-in closets, and the biggest bathroom I'd ever seen. We could have square-danced in the immense shower that had a high window that filled the tiled space with light.

"The whole house is perfect," Bill said. "See—" he'd opened a double-door closet in the master bath "—there's even a laundry area."

Natalie had caught up with us. "And it also has a double lot and a detached two-car garage. And a huge backyard beyond the courtyard with room for a pool and a vegetable garden."

Bill was looking more smitten by the minute. Natalie must have noticed, because she abandoned her sales pitch and disappeared again. She didn't need to be there. The house was selling itself.

Excited as a kid at a carnival, Bill tugged me back to the kitchen, out the back door, across the brick patio and through the gate in the courtyard fence. Natalie hadn't exaggerated about the backyard. There was a sunny expanse of Saint Augustine grass as well as areas shaded by live oaks and banked with azaleas. And several citrus trees loaded with fragrant blossoms grew near the garage. A ten-foot flowering viburnum hedge filled the air with fragrance and encompassed the property, providing quiet, privacy and a perch for a mockingbird that was singing his heart out, the only sound besides the rustle of a breeze.

After exploring every corner of the yard and the garage, Bill returned to where I'd found a seat on a stone retaining wall.

"Well," he said, "what do you think?"

"It's the first house we've looked at."

"But do you like it?"

I was suffering from a strange ambivalence. Part of me wanted to move in today, but another part, the commitment-scares-the-crap-out-of-me half, was terrified. I deflected his question with another. "What do you think?"

"The house and yard are filled with light, and—this might sound crazy, but—it's got good vibes, as if the people who've lived here have been happy." He glanced around, taking in everything. "It feels like home. A home I want to share with you, Margaret. But only if you like it, too," he added hastily.

I envied Bill. He wasn't an impulsive kind of guy. Most of his decisions were made slowly and methodically. But he also had the capacity to make instantaneous choices in the blink of an eye, instinctively acting in a manner that time proved to be correct. He wanted this house. He could already see himself—us—living here. I'd bet he was even arranging furniture in his head.

I, on the other hand, was the type who would dilly-dally for weeks, look at dozens of houses, and still be no more certain that I was doing the right thing when I finally made a choice.

"Well, what did y'all decide?" Natalie had tracked us down in the backyard.

Bill looked at me, hope shining in his baby blues. I looked at Natalie.

"We don't even know what it costs," I said.

She quoted the listing price, and I was glad I was sitting down.

"That much?" I gasped.

"Home prices have increased seventy percent since 1999," she said. "And here along the coast, they're only going to go higher. The sooner you buy, the more money you'll save."

"I can afford it," Bill assured me. "The important thing is whether you like it."

Bill wasn't blowing hot air. He'd worked his entire life earning only a cop's salary, but he would inherit thousands of acres of citrus groves near Plant City when his father, in his late eighties and the final stages of Alzheimer's, died. The Malcolm land was already worth millions and increasing in value every day.

Which put the ball in my court. The house was perfect, we could afford it, and Bill was obviously crazy about it. I swallowed my fears and misgivings. If this house would make Bill happy, that alone was reason enough to take the plunge. The fact that I liked it, too, was the clincher. "Let's make an offer."

"Woo-hoo!" Bill swung me off my feet and twirled me around the yard.

"I'll fill out the paperwork," Natalie said, "and you can meet me in the kitchen."

She left us again, and Bill stood with his arms around me while he surveyed his new domain. "We're going to be happy here, Margaret. I can feel it already."

I was beginning to feel it, too.

"It is close to the office and the marina," I said.

"But the best part is that it seems made for us," Bill said. "Can't you sense it?"

I could. Walking back through the courtyard and into the house felt like coming home.

* * *

Later, back in my condo after a late lunch at Dock of the Bay and a long nap, I was suffering the pangs of post-act dissonance. Without the peace and charm of the Cape Cod house working its magic, I couldn't help wondering if we'd been too hasty in plopping down a deposit on the first property we'd seen.

And, to be honest, I was worried about living with Bill anywhere. Even as a child, I'd always had my own room. In college, Daddy had insisted that I have my own apartment. After graduation, I'd never had a roommate either, and after flying solo for almost five decades, I feared ruining the best relationship of my life by too much togetherness.

I was remembering horror stories I'd heard about marriages that went south because one person squeezed the toothpaste tube in the middle, left the toilet seat up or dirty socks under the bed, when the phone rang and interrupted my angst session.

It was Adler.

"Did someone ID Deirdre's killer?" I asked.

I heard him release a breath in a whoosh. "The

sketches didn't look familiar to anyone, but we have a bigger problem now."

"Bigger than Deirdre's killer on the loose?"

"As big. Sidney Branigan's been murdered."

CHAPTER 18

"What?" I didn't think I'd heard Adler right.

"His wife found him shot to death in the driveway in front of his house. Crime techs are working the scene. I'm there now."

The wheels in my brain spun, working hard to assimilate this new development into a case that so far had made no sense. "Mind if I come over and butt in?"

"A fresh pair of eyes wouldn't hurt. Bring Malcolm, too."

"He's in Tampa, visiting his father, but I'll be there in ten minutes."

The ride to Harbor Oaks took fifteen, but Sidney Branigan wasn't going anywhere. He was sprawled on the driveway with a gunshot wound to the back of the head. When I arrived, Doc Cline was performing her initial examination. With the sun already set, the techs had erected portable tree lights to illuminate the crime scene, and several of the CSU team were combing the area.

I left my car parked on the street and met Adler at the foot of the driveway.

"What have you got?" I asked.

"No sign of robbery. The vic's still wearing his Rolex and a multicarat diamond ring and has almost a thousand in cash in his wallet."

"No witnesses?"

Adler shook his head. "From what we've been able to reconstruct, Sidney went to his mother's house around six to tell her goodbye."

"He and his family were still leaving on vacation in the morning?"

He nodded. "According to Stella Branigan, Sidney left her house about six-thirty. Madison, who showed him out, confirms that. Angela called Stella at seven to ask if Sidney was still there. When Stella told her how long he'd been gone, Angela came outside to look for him and discovered the body. That's when she called 911. Porter's doing in-depth interviews with the wife and house-keeper now."

"You'd better look hard at Angela," I said. "Re-member my feeling that there was tension in the family?"

Adler scratched his earlobe. "Angela and Ingrid have alibied each other. They were in the kitchen, fixing dinner, the whole time Sidney was gone. Brianna backs that up, too. She was with them, watching television. Porter's talking to them one at a time, to see if their initial stories hold up under scrutiny."

Doc approached us and peeled off her latex gloves. "I put time of death around six-thirty, give or take fifteen minutes. Looks like a small-caliber entry wound. Close range. I'll know more after the autopsy."

"In the morning?" Adler asked.

Doc shook her head. "Tonight. Our office is backed up, so most of us are putting in overtime. I might as well get this over with."

"I'll meet you at your office in an hour," Adler said.

"Guess that rules out lunch tomorrow," I said to Doc.

She laughed at our standing joke. "The first thing on my list when I retire is to have lunch with you, Maggie—if you've retired by then, too."

Even long hours hadn't taken the bounce out of her step as she turned toward the M.E.'s van, where her assistant was unloading a gurney with a body bag, and she hurried to help him.

"We have several uniforms canvassing the neighbors," Adler said, "but as secluded as this yard is, I doubt anyone saw anything."

I surveyed the scene. Perfectly trimmed head-high hedges hid the house and driveway from the street. And the street itself, while lined with streetlights, had a series of deep pockets of darkness cast by the massive trees that gave Harbor Oaks its name. Someone could have waited for Sidney in the shadows, shot him and slipped away into the gloom without ever being seen. As far apart as these homes were, if the neighbors had windows closed and televisions on, no one would have heard a shot.

"What's your take on this, Maggie?" Adler asked.

"It appears that someone has a vendetta against the Branigan family."

"Elaine Fisk?"

I shook my head. "She's in Pennsylvania. Deirdre's funeral was yesterday, and Elaine's staying to sort through Deirdre's belongings and put the family home on the market. And Elaine had an alibi for the time of Carlton's death, too."

Adler thought for a moment. "Maybe she hired a hit man."

"The girl's in a low-end job that earns barely enough to pay her bills. She can't afford a hit man."

"She could if she took out a mortgage on the family home."

I considered the possibility. "You can check that angle, but it still doesn't feel right. I've been so fixated on catching the killer in my cold cases, I could have drawn connections between Deirdre and the Branigans that weren't there. Maybe we haven't looked hard enough into Carlton Branigan's background for an enemy who's set on rubbing out his entire clan."

Adler glanced at his watch. "I should check with Porter, then get on over to the M.E.'s office. Want to come?"

The case had my head spinning, and I felt suddenly tired, in spite of my earlier nap. As much as I wanted to catch a killer, I couldn't think clearly until I'd had some rest. "No, thanks. Give me a call in the morning if you have anything new."

The next morning I arrived at the office late after sleeping in. When I brought Bill up to speed on Sidney's murder, he listened to what I was saying, but I could tell he was distracted. He looked as if he hadn't rested well.

"Tough visit with your dad yesterday?" I asked.

He nodded. "You remember what he was like before?"

I pictured Bill's dad when I had first met him more than twenty years ago. In his sixties then, he'd been an active, vibrant man, a big, rawboned citrus grower, his skin weathered by too much sun, his smile warm and his disposition as sweet as the oranges he'd grown. I'd liked him instantly, recognizing where Bill had inherited his powerful charisma. "I remember."

"You wouldn't recognize him now. His body's shriveled as badly as his mind. It's hell to watch him wasting away before my eyes. The only consolation is knowing that he's unaware of what's happening to him." Bill turned from the window he'd been staring out and locked his gaze with mine. "This stuff could be hereditary, you know."

I felt as if someone had squeezed my heart in a steel fist. "Or merely the result of statistics. Anyone who lives past eighty-five has a fifty-fifty chance of developing Alzheimer's."

"That's why I'm counting on us buying that house, Margaret. We're not getting any younger, and I don't want to waste a second of the time we have left."

Just the thought of a life without Bill in it brought a lump to my throat, but before I could say anything, Darcy appeared at the door.

"Mrs. Branigan's on the line, Maggie. She wants to talk to you."

"Which Mrs. Branigan?"

"The old one."

Darcy returned to the reception area, and I gave Bill a quick kiss before going to my desk in the other room to answer the phone.

"I'm sorry about Sidney, Mrs. Branigan," I said when I picked up.

"Thank you." Her voice sounded strained, but

then she'd lost her husband and her only child in the space of a few days. I didn't expect her to sound normal.

"Sidney's murder is a terrible shock," she said in a trembling tone. "At least Carlton was spared this."

"I need to talk with you. May I come over this morning?"

"No," Stella said quickly. "That's why I called. I'm terminating your employment."

I hadn't expected to be fired, but figured she probably blamed me for Sidney's death. After all, if his killer was the same as his father's and I'd been successful in tracking him down, her son would still be alive.

"I understand what you're feeling," I said, "but I'm concerned for your safety."

"Why?"

"If whoever killed your husband and son has a gripe against your family, your life could be in danger."

There was a long pause on the other end of the line. "I'm perfectly safe," she said, more as if convincing herself than me. "I have Madison and a state-of-the-art alarm system."

I pictured Carlton and Sidney, both murdered in their own yards. "You can't stay inside forever."

"As soon as Sidney's had a proper burial, I'm leaving for Europe. This place has too many painful memories." Her voice sounded tearful now, as if she was about to lose control.

"Can you think of anyone," I said, "who'd have reason to harm Carlton and Sidney?"

Her sigh of frustration reverberated through the line. "I've told the police everything I know, which isn't much. What do I owe you? I'll put a check in the mail."

I had no idea how many hours to bill her without calculations. "I'll have my secretary mail you an invoice."

"Fine," Stella said, and hung up.

I looked up to find Bill standing in the doorway. "We just lost a client."

"Stella Branigan?" He frowned. "That doesn't make sense. You'd think she'd want us to double our efforts now that her son's been killed."

I reached into my desk drawer for Benadryl gel to rub on the hives erupting on my forearms. "Nothing about these murders make sense."

"So maybe we're going at them from the wrong angle."

"Tell me another angle and I'll gladly try it."

Before Bill could make a suggestion, Darcy rang me on the intercom. "Adler wants to talk to you."

I picked up the phone.

"Can you and Malcolm meet Porter and me for lunch?" he said. "We want to brainstorm. Maybe we can jump-start these stalled investigations."

"Hold on." I covered the receiver and looked at Bill. "Lunch with Adler?"

Bill nodded.

I spoke into the phone. "How about Dock of the Bay?"

"Great," he said. "One o'clock? That'll give us time to canvass Sidney's neighbors again, in case they've remembered something they forgot to tell us last night."

"Have you finished working the bars with the sketch of Deirdre's killer?"

"While we cover this latest case, Mary Garrabrant and her partner are distributing the sketches."

"Anything I can do?"

"Not for now," Adler said. "See you at one."

I hung up and looked at Bill, who'd settled into the club chair across from my desk. "We've lost one client," I said, "Jolene's case is on hold until she returns from Cancún, and we've hit a wall on the Fisk murder. So what do we do now?"

"I have another workmen's comp case to follow up in Dunedin. Want to come?"

"Only if you buy me coffee on the way." I figured if I tagged along, I could keep Bill's mind off his father with my sparkling conversation and rapier wit.

And being with Bill might keep me from banging my head against the wall in frustration.

CHAPTER 19

By one o'clock, the Dock of the Bay was crowded with regulars and tourists, so Bill and I sat on the dock behind the restaurant instead of our usual booth. The rustic wooden structure extended over the waters of the marina and was filled with teak chairs and tables shaded by colorful market umbrellas. An exterior speaker piped music from the Wurlitzer inside, and Gretchen Wilson was belting out "Redneck Woman," her enthusiastic "hell, yeahs" punctuating the cries of gulls, the rustle of palm fronds and the gentle lap of waves against the pilings.

Bill ordered a beer, and I asked for a raspberry iced tea with lime. Adler and Porter arrived at the same time as our drinks. Once they'd placed their orders, we got down to business.

"New development," Adler said.

"Yeah," Porter added, "it's got us scratching our heads."

"New developments are good," I said. "Maybe they'll get this investigation moving."

"Or muddy the waters," Adler said. "I got a call a few minutes ago from the young hooker at the shelter. She was watching the noon news on TV and saw the coverage of Sidney's murder. The station broadcast file footage of Sidney taken during his father's last victory celebration."

"You're not going to believe this," Porter said with a drawl.

"Try us," Bill said.

"The hooker," Adler said, "fingered Sidney as Deirdre Fisk's killer."

I almost spewed my iced tea. "What?"

"Yup," Adler continued, "said she recognized him the minute she saw him cross the stage in the video."

"And she's positive?" Bill asked.

Porter nodded. "She's willing to swear to it in court."

"But why would Sidney kill Deirdre?" My mind was working to process this new information, but I was getting nowhere fast.

"What if Sidney was your child killer?" Porter said.

"He'd have been a teenager at the time," Bill noted, "but that doesn't rule him out."

I shook my head. "It doesn't fit. Deirdre went looking for someone she'd recognized in the news photo. Sidney wasn't pictured, his father was. And Sidney looks like his mother, not his father."

"While you're mulling that over—" Adler dug into the breadbasket the waitress had placed on the table and slathered butter on a roll "—throw this into the mix. We got the ballistics report on the bullet that killed Sidney."

Porter waved away a gull making a swooping pass at the breadbasket. "The .22 that killed Sidney was fired from the same gun as the bullet that killed Deirdre."

"Whoa, back up," I said. "The hooker says Sidney killed Deirdre, but, according to the ballistics report, the gun he used on her was also used to kill him?"

Adler nodded and reached for another roll.

"Did you do a search of Sidney's house last night?" Bill asked.

"House, garage and yard," Adler said. "But no sign of a gun."

"We did find gardening gloves with stains on the palms," Porter said. "CSU is processing them now."

That snippet made me sit up and take notice. "You think they're the gloves Carlton's killer wore?"

"Time will tell," Adler said, "whether the stains are blood and if it belonged to Branigan Senior."

Porter bit into his own roll and chewed. "Maybe Angela found out that Sidney had been a sexual predator and killed her husband in a rage. Maybe he'd even molested his own daughter, and Angela offed him to protect Brianna."

Adler shook his head. "The housekeeper swears Angela didn't leave the house last night until mere minutes before she found Sidney. According to Doc's timetable, Sidney had been dead half an hour when Angela found him."

"Have you done polygraphs on Angela and Ingrid?" Bill asked.

"Next step," Adler said.

A boat in a nearby slip started its engines and filled the air with noise and diesel fumes as it backed slowly into the channel. Adler took advantage of the interruption to keep eating. I tried to think above the din.

The facts didn't fit. I felt as if we were trying to

work a puzzle by hammering in the wrong-shaped pieces. "If Sidney killed Deirdre, who killed Carlton? And why?"

"Carlton could have found out about Sidney's perversion," Adler said. "When he confronted his son, Sidney snapped and strangled his old man."

The waitress arrived with a tray filled with our orders, and Bill waited until she had set our plates in front of us and moved away before asking his question. "How would Carlton have discovered that Sidney was a pervert?"

"The senator was out of town when Deirdre was killed," I reminded them.

"Maybe Stella knows more than she's saying," Porter suggested.

I shook my head. "From what I've learned about Stella and her worship of Carlton, I doubt she'd protect Sidney if she knew he'd killed his father. She doesn't seem the maternal type."

"But she could be hiding something," Bill said, "and that would explain why she took us off Carlton's case this morning."

"And why she's leaving the country after Sidney's funeral," I added.

Adler raised his eyebrows. "Stella fired you? And she's leaving town? Interesting." He was already halfway through his burger and attacking a mountain of French fries. "These killings keep getting more tangled. At least we've solved Deirdre's murder."

Porter lifted his iced tea. "To a closed case."

I joined in the toast and caught Bill's eye as he raised his longneck. Like me, he didn't look convinced.

When I returned to the office, I called Doc Cline and asked her to compare Sidney's DNA as well as his father's to the sample from my Tampa cold cases. If Sidney had killed the Tampa children, that fact would put an entirely new twist on the case.

With nowhere to go in my investigations until I heard back from Doc and from Archer Phillips on his data search, I bit the bullet and went to visit Mother.

Estelle answered the door.

"Is she awake?" I asked, and felt a stab of guilt at my hope for a negative reply.

"She's sitting in the courtyard. Go on in and I'll bring you both something cool to drink."

Estelle turned toward the kitchen, and I passed through the living room to the central courtyard of the two-story house. An arching glass ceiling protected the expanse from rain and kept in the air-conditioning. Mother didn't hear my approach over the splashing of the mosaic-tiled fountain, and I spoke before I reached her to keep from startling her.

"Hello, Mother. Good book?"

She set aside the volume she'd been reading, removed her glasses and made a face. "Why every story nowadays has to be filled with sex and violence, I'll never understand."

She formed her sentences slowly and with care. Those actions and a subtle slurring of her words were the only remaining traces of her stroke.

I sat in the wrought-iron chair beside her. Its plump cushions made it comfortable as well as attractive. "I can recommend some tamer reading. You might like Jan Karon's Mitford books."

I hadn't had time to read them, but they'd been highly recommended by Darcy and my friend Karen Longwood.

"Ah, Margaret," Mother said with a sigh, "you

should have remained a librarian. Your life is as rough as these books I can't read."

"Real life often isn't pretty." I resisted the urge to defend my chosen profession. I'd tried too many times in the past and failed.

"I know I've led a sheltered life," she surprised me by saying. "I've been lucky in that respect."

"How are you feeling?"

"Better. This episode has given me lots of time to think."

Estelle appeared with a tea tray that held glasses of lemonade and a plate of homemade sugar cookies. She placed them on the table next to Mother, shot me an encouraging smile behind Mother's back and hobbled away on her bunion-afflicted feet.

Mother handed me a glass and passed the cookies. I took one, and the first bite reminded me of afternoons with Estelle in the big kitchen when I'd arrived home from school.

"So, Mother, what have you been thinking about?" I braced myself for an in-depth description of some upcoming social extravaganza.

"I've been thinking about you."

Oh, boy. I would have preferred the tedium of

Pelican Bay's social calendar to a litany of my shortcomings.

"Seton said," Mother continued, "that if Estelle hadn't reacted so quickly to my illness, I might have died. That's a sobering realization, and it's had me reevaluating many things in my life."

I had no idea where she was headed, so I sipped my lemonade and nodded.

"I'm afraid I haven't been a very good mother to you," she said with unfamiliar humility.

Stunned by her admission, I could think of no response.

"But I intend to make it up to you," she continued, "as much as I can in the time that I have left."

Her unexpected sentiments brought tears to my eyes. "You needn't worry about me, Mother. Just concentrate on staying healthy."

She shook her head. "I've been too hard on you, Margaret, dear. I had my own expectations for you, and when you didn't meet them, I held that against you."

She had me now. I couldn't deny what she'd said, but I didn't dare agree, either. Mother had never taken kindly to criticism.

"So I've decided to change my ways," she said with the enthusiasm of someone swallowing a bitter dose of medicine that was supposed to be good for her.

"What do you mean?"

"I want to take a more active part in your life."

"Hmm," I said in a neutral tone and took another swallow of lemonade. As much as I'd always longed for her acceptance, more of Mother in my life was a change I could do without.

"And I've decided the perfect way to prove my good intentions," she said.

I was afraid to ask. "What's that?"

She smiled, and her eyes sparkled. "I'm going to give you the biggest wedding Pelican Bay has ever seen."

Luckily I had a good grip on my glass or it would have smashed against the terra-cotta tiles of the courtyard. I opened my mouth to tell her that Bill and I had agreed on a simple and private civil ceremony, but the words wouldn't come.

All my life I'd wanted Mother's approval, and now that she seemed on the verge of bestowing it, I couldn't automatically reject her. February, after all, was ten months away, and Mother could change her mind by then.

I forced a smile. "I'm glad you're feeling well enough to be making plans. That's a good sign."

She nodded. "I have to start right away. February will be here before you know it, and there are a thousand details to attend to."

Chicken that I was, I held my tongue. I'd wait a week or two until Mother was stronger. Then I'd put a lid on her grandiose wedding plans.

The message light on my answering machine indicated I'd had callers when I returned home. I pushed Play and heard Archer Phillips's voice.

"I have your info on Carlton Branigan, Margaret. Give me a call. Better yet, come by the office and bring a check."

CHAPTER 20

Too curious to wait for the drive into Clearwater, I rang Archer back.

"What did you find?" I asked after working my way past his mother, who screened all his calls.

"Carlton Branigan's whereabouts are unaccounted for on the nights those girls were murdered in Tampa," Archer said. "No meetings or public appearances on record. That doesn't mean he was out stalking children, though. He could have been at home with his family, but we'd have no record of that."

"What about his car? Did you find out what he was driving back then?"

"A white Cadillac Coupe DeVille."

Deirdre had described her assailant as driving a big white car, but Sidney would have been old enough for a license back then, and Daddy might have loaned him the keys.

"Did you find any mention of Sidney during that time?'"

"The son? He was still in high school, a private one in Tampa, and living at home."

"Thanks, Archer. I appreciate your help."

"I'm going to need more than appreciation. You owe me another five hundred."

"The check's in the mail," I said, and hung up.

No sooner had I returned the handset to its cradle than the phone rang again.

It was Adler. "Got the lab report back on those garden gloves. They're the same make as the fibers we found on Carlton's body. The stains are a mixture of chlorophyll and Carlton's blood. And that's not all. Inside the gloves, we found skin cells belonging to Sidney. Looks like Sidney killed his old man."

The pieces were coming together, but the picture still wasn't clear. "The question is why? Was Carlton molesting his granddaughter? Or was Sidney the pervert and Carlton found out about it?"

"If we can answer that question," Adler said, "we'll know who killed Sidney."

"Do you have an address for Ingrid, the house-keeper?"

"Sure." I heard the pages of his notebook rustling. "She lives in Pelican Bay in a mobile home park near downtown." He gave me the street address.

"Has she taken her polygraph yet?"

"It's scheduled for tomorrow."

"I think I'll pay Ingrid a visit."

"Okay by me," Adler said. "Let me know if you learn something useful."

"Deal," I said. "By the way, you searched Stella's house after Carlton was killed, didn't you?"

"Yeah, we were looking for gloves or bloody clothes. Found nothing."

"Any sign of a .22 handgun?"

"Nope," Adler said. "No guns of any kind in the house."

"And no gun found at Sidney's place?"

"Nope, but I have divers checking the harbor along the Branigan properties today in case the killer pitched the murder weapon into the water. The chief's getting pressure from the governor to solve Carlton's murder, so we've been given unlimited resources."

"Ain't politics grand," I said with a sigh.

"Hey, whatever works."

"Keep me posted," I said, and hung up.

A few minutes later I was driving east on Main Street to Palm Haven Mobile Home Park. Unlike many older parks, with rusted-out trailers and residents down on their luck, Palm Haven was a new facility filled with up-to-date, spacious manufactured homes with modern charm and conveniences. The park's only similarity to its seedier counterparts was its narrow lots that gave neighbors sweeping vistas of one another's windows.

When I pulled in front of the address Adler had given me, Ingrid was stowing a suitcase in the trunk of her car. I left my Volvo and approached her.

"Leaving town?" I asked.

She jumped, apparently so preoccupied she'd been unaware of my arrival. "I'm moving in with Miss Angela and Brianna for a while. Poor things, all alone in that big house."

"May I ask a few questions first? I won't take much of your time."

Ingrid slammed the trunk. "All right. Will you come in?"

I followed her into the mobile home, whose cathedral ceiling and tall windows made it sunny and inviting.

"Would you like some tea?" she asked.

I shook my head. "Just some information. I'm trying to find Sidney's killer, and I need your help."

She pointed to a chair, and I sat. She settled on the end of the sofa nearest me. "I told the detectives. We were all in the kitchen and didn't see or hear anything."

Her face was puffy, as if she'd been crying, but her body language was relaxed, proclaiming she had nothing to hide.

"Can you tell me why Brianna didn't want to spend time with her grandparents?"

Color flooded her features, and she clasped her hands tightly in her lap. "It's not my place to talk about that."

"We need all the facts to solve these murders."

"But I'm not supposed to know." Ingrid's lower lip quivered, and she was obviously fighting back tears.

"Know what?" I asked with all the gentleness I could muster.

"About poor little Brianna. I overheard her parents arguing."

I was getting nowhere fast, so I cut to the chase. "Was her father molesting her?"

"Her father?" Ingrid snapped up her head in astonishment. "Absolutely not! Her father would never—it was the old man."

"Carlton Branigan?"

She nodded. "That's why Angela and Brianna had gone to Miss Angela's parents the morning the senator was murdered—because the senator was coming home. They wanted to keep Brianna away from him."

"Her parents knew he'd been molesting Brianna and they did nothing?"

Ingrid shook her head. "They didn't know until the night before. Brianna had been acting strangely for months, not wanting to visit next door, begging to stay home. The night before the senator returned for spring break, she finally broke down and told her parents what that sick old man had been doing to her."

I felt sick myself. "You're certain of this?"

"I wish I wasn't. As I said, I'm not supposed to know, but with so much turmoil in that house, it was impossible not to hear."

I thanked her and left.

* * *

With the office less than a mile away, within minutes, I was at my desk and telling Bill what I'd learned.

Bill lost his usual calm, and his face was suffused with anger. "God, you get used to some awful things in this business, but a man molesting his own grandchild? It makes me want to throw up."

"It definitely gives Sidney motive to kill his old man. But with both of them dead and no witness to their confrontation, I guess we'll never know whether Sidney inadvertently strangled Carlton in a fit of rage or went next door planning to kill him."

Darcy buzzed me on the intercom. "Doc Cline's on the line."

I picked up the phone with a pretty good idea of what the medical examiner was going to tell me.

"I did those DNA comparisons," Doc said. "According to the samples from your cold case, Carlton Branigan was the man who molested and murdered those three young girls in Tampa."

I thanked her and hung up.

My reaction to Doc's news was a curious mix of satisfaction and regret. Pleased that the cases that had haunted me so long were finally solved, I was sorry that Carlton was dead, denying me the pleasure of seeing him prosecuted to the full extent of the law. Florida, after all, still had the death penalty.

Being brutally murdered at the hands of his son was a horrible punishment, but the public humiliation of a trial would have been worse for a man like Carlton.

"Carlton Branigan was the sexual predator who killed those little girls and abducted Deirdre sixteen years ago," I told Bill. "Doc matched the DNA samples."

Bill sat in the chair in front of my desk. "We should check with the Tallahassee police. The Tampa killings stopped shortly after Branigan was elected to the state legislature. I'm betting there are unsolved cases in the capital—or the outlying areas—which can now be traced to Carlton. Predators like him don't quit. They just change territory."

"So now we know who killed Deirdre Fisk and Sidney," I said.

Bill nodded. "The problem is proving it."

CHAPTER 21

Bill and I were waiting for Elaine Fisk at the Tampa International Airport concourse when she returned from Pennsylvania the following morning. We led her to a booth in the rear of Ruby Tuesday's and, over breakfast, told her our suspicions and our plan.

"I want to catch Deirdre's killer." Elaine pushed aside the omelet she'd barely touched, cradled her coffee mug in her hands and gazed at us over its rim. "But is what you're suggesting legal? I don't want to do anything that will jeopardize a conviction."

"We're not with the police," Bill explained, "so technically, entrapment's not an issue."

I drained the last of my coffee. "You ready to make the call?"

"Let's do it," Elaine said with a resolute nod.

Bill stood and grabbed the check. "There's a bank of pay phones just around the corner from the restaurant. You can call from there."

While Bill paid the cashier, Elaine and I went outside and chose a phone at the end of the row that was fairly secluded from the others. I dialed the number, and when our suspect answered, handed Elaine the phone.

She took a deep breath and grasped the receiver so hard her knuckles whitened. "This is Elaine Fisk, Deirdre's sister. I've found something you might be interested in."

Bill had joined us, and Elaine glanced at us with a hint of panic. He patted her shoulder, and I gave a nod of encouragement.

"I just finished going through Deirdre's belongings," Elaine continued. "She has newspaper photos and a journal that identify the man who abducted her in Tampa years ago. If you don't want them, I'm taking them to the police and the media."

The person on the other end of the line spoke, and Elaine shook her head. "No, I haven't told anyone. And I won't tell anyone—for the right price."

She listened again. "That sounds fair. I'll trade you what I have for cash." Another pause. "Yes, I know the place. Midnight? I'll be there."

Elaine replaced the receiver and wiped her perspiring palm on the front of her blouse. "It's all set. In the park tonight, the same spot where Deirdre was killed."

"Thanks," I told her. "We'll let you know what happens."

"Stay safe," she said. "You know you're dealing with a cold-blooded killer."

"One you will have helped put behind bars," I said.

With a sad little smile, she turned and crossed the concourse to the escalators that descended to the luggage carousels.

"Let's get moving," Bill said. "We have purchases to make and a park to reconnoiter before dark."

At eleven o'clock, I inspected my appearance in the full-length mirror in my bedroom. Hip-hugging, bell-bottomed jeans, a tight little T-shirt that left my midriff bare, and clunky shoes resembled an outfit that Elaine might have worn. A wig of long, pale blond hair and sunglasses completed my disguise. In the bright lights of my condo, I looked like a joke, an older woman clinging too tightly to her long-vanished youth. In the dark at Crest Lake Park, I hoped I'd look enough like Deirdre's sister to fool our suspect.

After slipping my gun into a macramé shoulder bag, I called a cab.

Fifteen minutes later, I was walking toward the bench in the park where I'd met the young hooker a few days earlier. Tonight, at least, she was safe and secure in the shelter and, I hoped, working on getting her life back on track.

I settled on the bench, pulled a large manila envelope stuffed with blank paper from my purse, and propped it against my hip in plain sight. Now all I had to do was wait.

On the other side of the lake, traffic whizzed by on Gulf-to-Bay Boulevard, but the park itself was quiet. A slight breeze ruffled the surface of the lake and rustled the leaves of nearby shrubs. The plaintive call of a chuck-will's-widow broke the stillness. The air had turned cool with a late-season cold front, and I could feel goose bumps rising on my bare flesh. I slid my hand into my bag for a reassuring grip on the butt of my Smith & Wesson.

The clunk of a car door slamming carried on the night air, and I tensed in expectation. My eyes had adjusted to the gloom, and I could see a figure approaching on the sidewalk from the parking area. Tall with broad shoulders and an athletic stride, the newcomer was dressed exactly as the hooker had described. Loose trousers and long-sleeved shirt, a ball cap and sunglasses. If I hadn't known better, I'd have sworn Sidney Branigan had returned from the dead to meet me in the park.

Show time.

With my hand on the gun in my bag, I stood as the suspect approached. Everything seemed to break loose at once, then switched to such slow motion that I observed all that happened with stunning clarity. A gun appeared from the pocket of the loose slacks. Bill catapulted from the bushes by the sidewalk and took the suspect down. From their hiding place nearby, Adler and Porter leaped onto the path, secured the gun, made the arrest and Mirandized their captive.

In the tussle, the ball cap and sunglasses had been knocked aside. I stripped off my wig and glasses and faced Stella Branigan's unswerving, steely glare.

"You were supposed to be working for me," she said, her haughty demeanor undeterred by the handcuffs on her wrists.

"You fired me, remember?"

She turned her fury on Adler and Porter, who held her by the arms. "You have no right to arrest me. I've done nothing wrong."

Adler hefted the gun, a .22, which he'd stowed in an evidence bag. "For now, carrying without a permit will do. We'll throw the rest of the book at you later."

"Meet us at the station?" Porter said.

"We're right behind you," Bill answered.

The pair led Stella away, and Bill put his arm around my shoulders and squeezed. "I was worried about you. I'm glad this is over."

"I wasn't worried," I said.

"You should have been. Stella would have shot you if she'd had the chance."

"But she didn't." I gave him a kiss. "Because you had my back."

"I'd like to have the rest of you, too," he said with a grin.

"Later," I promised, "but first we have to see how well Stella Branigan sings."

* * *

Bill and I stood behind the one-way glass and watched Adler and Porter question Stella in the interview room. She had yet to request her lawyer, which I thought strange for a woman in her position, but, as the interview unfolded, her contorted reasoning and her increasing mental instability became clear.

Stella was either losing her grip on reality or was suffering under the delusion that the fewer people who knew about her husband's crimes, the less likely that the media would get hold of the facts.

She leaned across the table toward Adler and whispered, "I'm telling you all of this in confidence."

Adler glanced at Porter, who was leaning in the corner, one foot propped against the wall, his arms crossed over his chest, then returned his full attention to Stella.

"We're the only ones here," Adler assured her. "And things will go better for you if you cooperate and tell us everything."

"It all started with that horrible young woman." Stella spit the angry words, and a trickle of saliva appeared at the corner of her mouth. "She showed up on a Monday night, saying she needed to speak with Carlton. I thought she was a constituent, so I asked her in, even though Carlton was still in Tallahassee. When she saw his portrait above the mantel, she turned pale and started to hyperventilate. She was shaking hard, and when I asked what was wrong, she told the most horrible tale, made the most gruesome accusations, that I knew she had to be silenced."

Adler nodded in sympathy. "Deirdre's story would have ruined your husband's career."

"Exactly. I told her I couldn't talk at the house— I couldn't kill her in my own living room, could I? So I made up a story about Carlton coming home any minute and arranged to meet her in the park later. I promised her we'd go to the police together. But I knew she had to be stopped."

Stella's mental state was obviously becoming more and more fragile. The expression in her eyes was wild, furtive. Her hands plucked at her sleeves in mindless gestures. With her hair matted from the ball cap and her baggy, masculine attire, she looked nothing like the self-assured socialite I'd first met.

"How did you stop Deirdre?" Porter's question was offhand, almost nonchalant.

"I shot her."

"With the gun you had tonight?" Adler asked.

Stella nodded.

"We searched your house after your husband was murdered," Porter said. "The gun wasn't there."

Stella's smile was smug. "After I shot that horrible little Fisk woman, I put the gun in the safety-deposit box at the bank. I didn't get it out again until after my house had been searched."

"You know that Sidney killed his father?" Adler asked.

Stella's smile crumpled into grief. "I didn't know until Sidney told me Sunday night. He killed his own father for no reason." With her expression pleading, she reached across the table and grabbed Adler's arm. "Carlton would never touch Brianna, not in that way."

I turned to Bill. "Looks like Stella is the Queen of de Nile."

"Or has lost all her marbles," he said. "If she had no idea what Carlton's been up to all these years, the shock of Deirdre's story and Sidney's accusations could have sent her over the edge."

Adler gently disengaged Stella's death grip from his arm.

"Were you afraid Sidney would tell on his father?" Porter was asking.

Stella shook her head. "He wanted to protect Brianna. He would never have said anything to anybody."

"Then why did he confess to you?" Porter said.

Stella began to shiver. She hugged herself and rocked slowly back and forth in her chair. "He said he was sick of hearing me say how wonderful his father was, that it was time I knew the truth." She rocked harder. "But it wasn't the truth. It was all lies."

"Is that why you killed your son?" Adler asked in a soft voice. "To stop the lies?"

She stopped her swaying movement and shook her head. Her eyes flashed fire and her lips curled in a snarl. "I didn't mean to kill him, just to frighten him to protect his father's memory. Carlton was the best man in the whole world. He would have been governor someday. Maybe even president. He'd worked toward that goal his entire life, and Sidney was going to ruin Carlton's good name. It was all so horribly unfair. But Sidney wouldn't listen and the gun went off...." She folded her arms on the table, lowered her head and sobbed.

With three recent murders and three cold cases solved, I had expected a sense of satisfaction, but all I felt was sadness and fatigue.

"I've seen enough," I said to Bill. "Let's go home."

CHAPTER 22

Two days later, Bill, reading the *Times*, sat in the club chair at the office with his feet propped on my desk. Yesterday we'd been deluged with calls from the media for details on the now-solved cold cases, the Fisk and Branigan murders, and our capture of Stella Branigan. Nothing stirs the juices of an investigative reporter better than the fall of the mighty.

"At least we got some good plugs for Pelican Bay Investigations," Bill said, "and right on the front page. That'll help business."

"We're already too busy," I said. "We need a break."

Bill dropped the paper to his lap and stared at me in surprise. "Is that Margaret the workaholic talking? I can't believe my ears."

"I'm learning to slow down," I said.

He nodded in approval. "Let's take a trip. How about a few days on Sanibel?"

"Sound great—oh, no."

"What?"

"I forgot about Jolene and Gracie. I have to wrap that situation up first, but Jolene should be back from Cancún by now."

Bill's cell phone rang, and he pulled it from his pocket and answered. The longer he listened, the more his smile broadened.

"Thanks," he said, "we'll be in touch."

"Good news?" I asked.

"The best. That was Natalie Pettigrew, the Realtor. We got the house."

"Wow." I'd been so focused on the recent murders, I'd forgotten all about the charming Cape Cod cottage in Adler's neighborhood.

"We close in three weeks," Bill said. "Now all we need is—"

"A dog?" Darcy stood in the doorway.

Bill shook his head. "Furniture."

"Well," Darcy said, "you got a dog."

I started to speak but something warm and furry

attached itself to my leg beneath my desk. I pushed back my chair and gazed down into the upturned face of Roger, the pug, his expression blissful and adoring.

"Roger!" I scooped him into my arms and looked to Darcy. "What's he doing here?"

Darcy rolled her eyes. "Gracie Lattimore just dropped him off. Said you could have him."

"Call Jolene Jernigan," I said. "Tell her I'll bring him right over."

Bill had come over and was scratching Roger behind his ears. "Hey, fellow."

Roger was loving it.

"Jolene's gone back to New York," Darcy said.

"Without Roger?"

Darcy nodded. "With Gracie and Ed, Jolene's new hunk of burning love, who, it seems, is allergic to dogs. Jolene told Gracie to take Roger to the pound, but Gracie didn't have the heart."

"Why didn't Gracie talk to me?" I asked.

"She was in too big a hurry, but said to tell you that everything has worked out fine. The limo was waiting outside to take them to the airport. Jolene goes back to work tomorrow."

"Thanks, Darcy." I shook my head at the most

recent turn of events, and Darcy returned to her office.

Roger leaped from my arms, then jumped from the floor to a chair and onto a low bookcase beneath the window. After turning around a few times, he settled down and stared at the cars and people passing on the street below.

"We can find him a good home," I said.

"I like dogs," Bill said, "and Roger certainly likes you."

What the hell, I thought. I'd committed to marriage and buying a house. I might as well have a dog, too.

"With Jolene's case closed," Bill said, "we can sail to Sanibel today."

I grinned. "We'll have our own spring break."

Bill put his arms around me and pulled me close. "When I'm with you, I feel like a college kid again. Maybe you should pack those hip-hugger jeans and that skimpy little shirt you wore the other night."

I kissed the tip of his nose. "Feeling like a college kid and *looking* like a college kid are two entirely different animals."

"Speaking of animals, we'll need a life vest for Roger."

"Not to mention food, dishes and a bed."

"Taken care of," Darcy called from the reception area, which proved what I'd always suspected about her keen hearing and love of eavesdropping. "Gracie left all Roger's things, including his vet records and his dog license."

I sighed and said in a stage whisper, "Guess we'll have to give the help some time off, too."

"Wouldn't hurt," Bill said. "We need to stay on her good side, since she apparently knows all our secrets."

"I heard that," Darcy shouted.

"Ready for that vacation, Ms. Skerritt?" Bill offered me his arm.

"Ready." I looped my arm through his.

Roger barked and jumped from the bookcase.

"C'mon, boy," I said. "I hope you like boats."

"Of course, he likes boats," Bill insisted. "We'll get him an eye patch and call him Jolly Roger."

Darcy raised her eyebrows when we passed through her office. "When will you, Jimmy Buffett, and your little pirate be back?"

"No set time," Bill said quickly. "A few weeks or so."

"Shut down the office," I told her, "turn on the

answering machine, and go home. For now, we're all on spring break."

With Bill whistling, "Come back to Jamaica," and Roger trotting happily alongside, we left the building.

* * * * *

Be sure to look for more Maggie Skerritt mysteries,
only from Harlequin Next!

You're never too old to sneak out at night

BJ thinks her younger sister, Iris, needs a love interest. So she does what any mature woman would do and organizes an Over-Fifty Singles Night. When her matchmaking backfires it turns out to be the best thing either of them could have hoped for.

Over 50's Singles Night

by Ellyn Bache

HN37

Available April 2006
TheNextNovel.com

There are things inside us
we don't know how to express,
but that doesn't mean
they're not there.

A poignant story about a woman
coming to terms with her relationship
with her father and learning to open up
to the other men in her life.

The Birdman's Daughter

by Cindi Myers

HARLEQUIN®
NeXt™

Available April 2006
TheNextNovel.com

HN38

REQUEST YOUR FREE BOOKS!

2 FREE NOVELS TO INTRODUCE YOU TO OUR BRAND-NEW LINE!

There's the life you planned. And there's what comes next.

NEXT05

You always want
what you don't have

Dinah and Dottie are two sisters who grew up
in an imperfect world. Once old enough to make
decisions for themselves, they went their separate
ways—permanently. Until now. Will their reunion
seventeen years later during a series of crises
finally help them create a perfect life?

My Perfectly
Imperfect Life

Jennifer Archer

Available March 2006
TheNextNovel.com

HN34

A forty-something blushing bride?

Neely Mason never expected to walk down the aisle, but it's happening, and now her whole Southern family is in on the event. Can they all get through this wedding without killing each other? Because one thing's for sure, when it comes to sisters, *crazy* is a relative term.

The
GOOD KIND
OF CRAZY

TANYA MICHAELS

If her husband turned up alive—she'd kill him!

The day Fiona Rowland lifted her head above the churning chaos of kids, carpools and errands, annoyance turned to fury and then to worry when she realized Stanley was missing. Can life spiraling out of control end up turning your world upside right?

where's Stanley?

Donna Fasano

A Boca Babe
on a Harley?

Harriet's former life as a Boca Babe—where only looks, money and a husband count—left her struggling for freedom. Finally gaining control of her path, she's leaving that life behind as she takes off on her Harley. When she drives straight into a mystery that is connected to her past, will she be able to stay true to her future?

Dirty Harriet
by Miriam Auerbach

HN40

Available April 2006
TheNextNovel.com

HARLEQUIN®
NeXt™